Banff Springs Abbey

Samantha Adkins

Copyright © 2015 Samantha Adkins

All rights reserved.

ISBN: 1503251217
ISBN-13: 978-1503251212

DEDICATION

For my Mom, Jen, Julia, Megan and my JASNA Calgary friends.

ACKNOWLEDGMENTS

Jane Austen's Northanger Abbey is always surprising. I am continually delighted in and inspired by her works and hope she wouldn't mind me imaging her story in my own world.

With thanks to Jennifer Stromberg and Jim and Pat Karras for their editing assistance.

CHAPTER ONE

A noise echoed through Cate's head. She swatted it lazily with one hand, unwilling to leave her book. She hardly noticed, ensconced as she was in Diane Setterfield's world of ghosts and castles.

Her dark brown eyes ate up the words hungrily, aching to know what would happen next. Hoping to uncover secrets . . . and love.

"Catherine Julia Morland, you get into the kitchen this minute!" her mother's voice broke easily through her thin bedroom wall, but not so effortlessly through Cate's imagination.

Cate sat up with a jolt. Her mother must have been calling for a while to make it to her full name.

"Yes Mom!" she hollered, carefully placing a pressed-flower bookmark between the pages. "Coming!"

She hastily unwound her tangled ponytail and tried to smooth it back together while she hurried to the kitchen.

"Hi Mom. What do you need?" she said, a little unfocused after her hours between pages.

"Cate, where on earth have you been?" her mother's face was streaked with flour.

"Just in my room," Cate shrugged her shoulders in an attempt to look innocent.

"Reading again," her mother shook her head. "You're eighteen now, Cate. You can't just read all day."

Cate didn't see why not, but there was no use bringing that up now. "Did you need me for something?" Cate repeated.

"Yeah. You need to go get your brother. He's at Adam's house and he can't walk home alone."

"Sure Mom," Cate kissed her mother's cheek and left to get her jacket. The faster she did things, the less likely she was to get a lecture.

"Hurry home, Cate," her mother called as she left. "Supper's almost ready."

Cate stuffed her hands into her plaid jacket. It was too flimsy for the howling winter wind, but it was all she had. Her head felt stung by icicles the moment she stepped outside. She tried to hunch into her shoulders, but it didn't help.

The snow in front of their trailer home was patchy. Repeated thawing and freezing had turned it into a kind of powdered-ice garden. Her boots clicked against the slippery sidewalks which heaved in places, making it uneven. Adam's house was only a block from theirs. She didn't know why her brother couldn't walk home alone. He was seven already. She was pretty sure she walked farther when she was his age. But he was the baby.

A wind gust picked up a pile of icy dirt and hurtled it into Cate's eyes. She closed them against the assault, but it was too late for a few sharp pieces and tears instantly sprang to wash them away. Cate tripped then on one of the uneven sidewalk slabs and slipped off of her heeled, faux-leather boots. She landed on her backside with a thud.

"I hate it here!" she screamed into the unrepentant gale.

Strathmore was big enough to be called a city, officially, but the community had voted to remain a town. It had grown from about 3 000 to 12 000 residents in a short time and most of the people still believed they were living in a small town. There was nothing to do and nowhere to go and everyone hired their family members, which was fine if you didn't live with your Mom and three brothers in a trailer with no other relatives for miles. However, she did have one connection.

"Cate, we have exciting news. Text if you're still awake! Robin"

It was 9:30 on a Friday night. Only someone middle-aged would assume a 18-year-old girl would be asleep at that time. Even so, Cate had to lift her head off the bed where it had fallen half an hour before while she read.

"I'm awake!" Cate texted back. "What's up?"

Robin Allen had employed Cate's mother ever since her father died. Her mother had been a stay-at-home mom while her husband worked in the city. When the insurance money ran out, they sold their house for a trailer and the only work she could find was cleaning houses.

"We're planning a trip to Banff for Christmas break. Can you come?"

Cate looked quizzically at her nearly-dead cellphone. Why would they invite her on their vacation? Did they mean her whole family?

"I'll have to ask Mom. Do you want everyone or just me?"

The great thing about the Allen's was, even though they were wealthy and owned the biggest house in town, they treated them like family. If her mom didn't put her foot down, they would have bought them a house and a car and paid for everything they could want. Sometimes Cate wished her mom wasn't too proud to accept their generosity, but as she got older, she was starting to understand.

"Just you, honey. You're eighteen and you deserve a little holiday. I remember being your age!"

"Sounds awesome. I'll let you know."

Cate knew the Allen's paid her mother far more than any other house cleaners in the area. They also recommended her to several of their friends. The Allen's frequently invited the Morland family to barbeques, dinners and games nights. They didn't even seem to notice that Cate's family had nothing in common with their other friends and something about their warm hospitality helped their guests not to notice either – at least while they converged at the Allen house. Cate had learned quite young that if she approached these people at the Co-op to chat, they were quick to point out how urgently they needed to be somewhere else. Still, they didn't mind hiring Cate's mother to clean their homes.

Cate dropped her phone on her cozy, worn bedspread and wandered into the tiny living room to check with her mother. She was watching a Friday night Hallmark special with her eyes wide.

"Good show, Mom?" she asked.

"Shh. Sit down, you have to see this," Cate's mom patted the spot on the couch beside her.

Cate found Hallmark movies completely moronic. Overacting, thoughtless scripting and ridiculous plots made her want to scratch out her eyes, but she couldn't say no to her mom. Especially when she wanted to ask if it was okay to accept more of the Allen's generosity.

The husband in the movie was apparently keeping his new wife under close watch by secretly drugging her morning coffee. The wife thought she had cancer and was seeing a specialist to whom she felt strangely attracted. Then her husband started screening her phone calls and emails. Ooh, so scary.

The film ended with the wife safely in the arms of her doctor-lover and her husband dead in a lake. Her mother sighed contentedly and gave her a hug.

"It's nice to watch a movie with you," she said, sleepily.

"You too Mom." She waited a minute until her mom stood up to clear away a popcorn bowl and two pop cans.

"Mom, the Allen's invited me to go to Banff with them over Christmas," she said as she folded a blanket.

"What would we do without the Allens?" her mom's eyes grew a bit misty.

Cate stopped holding her breath. "Can I text back to say I can come?" Cate made a move toward her room.

"Oh, but it's so late. You don't want to disturb them. It's important we don't take advantage of them. You know, a lot of people do. I don't want us to be one of those mooches." Her mother sniffed with disgust. "And you should call them Cate. Texting is for friends and quick reminders between your family members. You need to show your appreciation for their offer with a good old-fashioned phone call."

"Okay, I'll call first thing in the morning," she said, almost out of the room.

"But not too early, Catherine. Tomorrow's a Saturday. You need to let them sleep in. Wait until ten, at least."

Cate did her best not to roll her eyes at her mother's social rules.

CHAPTER TWO

Cate woke at 5 a.m. the morning she was going to Banff. She kicked off her blankets like she hadn't since she was six. She pulled open her blinds and only laughed at the view of Mr. Duncan. Really, didn't he know her window looked right into his bathroom? She let the blinds drop again. She could look outside later.

The Allens had dropped off some luggage for her the night before. Cate flicked on her light switch to make sure they were real.

"It's just a little gift, Amy," Robin had told her mother when she dropped them off.

Cate's mom was busy racing around to pick up the odd pieces of lint from the surfaces in her house. She never had the Allens over and was obviously embarrassed that they showed up unannounced. The gifts just seemed to make things worse.

They had brought toys for Cate's brothers as well.

"We didn't want anyone to feel left out," Robin giggled. "I even got something for you!"

Robin handed over one more pink gift bag. Cate's mother's face seemed to match the cotton candy-coloured bag.

"You really shouldn't have," she muttered. She seemed afraid to look inside. Robin took care of that.

"Ta Da!" she held up an elegant suit. "I hope it fits. Gerald and I were thinking you might be ready to come work for us at the hotel. You must be tired of cleaning our house."

"Well, I don't know. . ."

"You don't have to decide right away. We'll meet in the New Year and talk it over. Maybe you have somewhere else you'd rather be."

"No, that's not it." Cate felt sorry for her humble mother.

"All of the gift receipts are in the bag," Robin continued. "I should have been practical and given you all gift cards, but I love to buy actual gifts, you know. It's so much more fun to imagine exactly what someone would like."

It seemed like Robin did in fact know precisely what each of the Morland family wanted. Cate's brothers were tearing through the house with their new nerf guns and Cate couldn't help touching her two new stylish pieces of luggage. Robin's husband, Gerald was much more reserved. He sat on their couch holding the mug of coffee Cate's mother had given him. He wasn't beaming like his wife, but he was easy to like.

"I'll just help Cate bring these to her room," Robin said, seeming to notice how flustered Cate's mother was.

Cate wasn't sure why she needed help. She could perfectly manage the bags herself, but when they came to her room, Robin closed the door behind her.

"I didn't want to overwhelm your Mom," she said in a loud whisper. "I tend to go overboard, but I must see your face when you open the suitcases." Robin clasped her hands excitedly.

"There's more?" Cate asked. "You really didn't need to get us anything. We should be thanking you for taking me to Banff."

"Oh, never mind that. We can't wait for you to come with us." Robin expertly unzipped the bags with her pale pink-manicured fingers. The suitcases were filled with clothing.

Cate gasped. "Robin! This is too much!"

"Just enough, by my count," she said. "We'll be gone for 10 days, so you'll need at least this many outfits. And the weather in Banff is always unpredictable, so you have enough clothes for all temperatures. And there's a dress for a special event, but I left that at our house. I didn't want it to get wrinkled in here." She patted the clothes.

Cate threw her arms around her friend. "Thank you, Robin. This is the nicest thing anyone has ever done for me."

Robin hugged her back and sniffed a little. "We never could have children of our own, so I hope you don't mind that we spoil you a little bit." She reached into her purse for a tissue. "Now come on, I want to see what you think of everything."

Robin started pulling out skirts and tops, sweaters and leggings. Cate held them up to her body and loved them all instantly. She rarely got new clothing and never so many at once. She couldn't help letting out a little whoop.

Now, Cate pulled on one top to wear for the drive. She smoothed her long, wavy brown hair and admired the well-fitting shirt which matched her dark colouring so well. She'd wear her old jeans, so her Mom wouldn't start asking questions. As far as she knew, Cate had only received the luggage. She still didn't know about the clothes. And the make up! Cate hadn't seen the make-up until the next day when she had gone through everything. There was a whole case of eyeliners, blush, eye shadow, lip glosses and mascara. She put on just a bit of mascara, trying to make it look as natural as possible. It made her brown eyes appear even larger.

By 5:30, she was showered, dressed and ready. Only 4 and a half hours to go! Why hadn't they decided to leave at 6? Cate paced her tiny room a few times, but then gave in and resumed reading The Thirteenth Tale.

"Here's a bit of money for the trip," Cate's Mom interrupted a few hours later.

"Oh Mom, I'm sure I don't need any more money. I've been saving up from baby-sitting and stuff."

Her mom sat on her bed, gazing at the luggage suspiciously. "Cate, the Allens are very generous people. I feel bad just sending you with them. Please don't let them spend too much on you. I have no way to repay them."

She fingered the zipper on one of the suitcases. Cate bit her lip, worried that her mother would open the bag.

"I'll do my best Mom. I won't even mention that I like things."

Her mom removed her hand from the bag and placed in on Cate's shoulder. "I know, honey. You've never been greedy. I'm just worried about you, I guess. I can't believe you'll be gone so long, and over Christmas too."

She hugged her mom. Things had been more difficult for her since Cate's big brother James had joined the army. Although he visited as often as he could, they missed his calming presence. Ever since Cate's dad died, James had done what he could to help at home. He was more responsible than any other 19-year-old's they knew and he had helped Cate and her three younger brothers with homework, friends and missing their Dad. He'd stayed an extra year after high school to help out, but after that, he needed to move on. They all missed him.

Cate held her phone in front of her mom's face. "You can text me any time. I'm not all that far away and I'm sure you won't miss cooking for one extra mouth."

Her mom tried to laugh, but it came out as more of a sob. She hugged her daughter one more time and then stood up, smoothing out her blue jeans. "I'm making blueberry pancakes," she said. "They'll be ready in about ten minutes."

"Thanks," Cate smiled and her mom left the room.

The Allens were early, thank goodness. Cate couldn't bear to look at her mom and see her trying so hard not to cry.

"Good morning to our favourite family!" Robin said when they entered their trailer-home. "Mmmm, it smells good in here."

"There are some pancakes left," Cate's mother said, sounding somewhat desperate. "Could you stay for a bit?"

Robin glanced at her husband with a questioning look. He smiled. "Well, we've already eaten, but maybe a cup of coffee would be nice."

Cate tried not to sigh, but she was anxious to go. She knew how long adults could make a cup of coffee last.

Cate's mother gasped. "I – I'm all out. I'm so sorry, I can just run to the store and buy another can. . ."

"Don't be silly, Amy. We always stop at Tim's on the way out of town. We'll have coffee when we come back."

Cate did a little dance in her imagination.

"Well, then, can I help you with your bags?" Gerald asked.

"Yes, thank you," Cate pointed out her suitcases and made sure to carry one herself. The faster she left the house, the faster they would begin their trip.

She felt a twinge of guilt when she waved goodbye to her mom and saw her three younger brothers chasing one another with their nerf guns through their muddy yard – there'd been a chinook and the snow had mostly melted now. Her mother would have to clean them up herself for the next five days, but her feelings of guilt subsided as soon as Gerald asked what she'd like to order from Tim Horton's.

"Hot chocolate and a Boston Cream donut, please," she said. Then she relaxed into her heated, cream-coloured leather seat and grinned with pleasure.

CHAPTER THREE

The foggy, grey Strathmore morning turned to sunshine as soon as they drove into Calgary. Robin played Simon and Garfunkel on her iPod and Cate sang along. It had been one of her dad's favourite albums.

"Are you sure you have enough clothes?" Robin asked when they drove past one of the large shopping malls.

"Yes!" Cate did her best to obey her mom's instructions.

Robin watched the mall pass with her lip between her teeth. "I don't know. Do you need anything, Gerald?"

Gerald grinned and put a hand on his wife's knee. "We have more than enough packed, honey. We're only going for 10 days and if you really need something, it's only an hour drive into the city."

Robin laughed at herself. "I just can't seem to pass by a mall without stopping. I think it comes from years of living in the country where you can hardly buy anything."

Cate watched the buildings zip by her windows. So much concrete.

"Enough of our fogey music, Cate. What do you want to listen to?" Gerald asked.

Cate was shy about sharing her music choices. She handed over her iPod. "Anything on here is good. Just pick something you like."

Robin sifted through the songs and landed on Hedley. "Oooh, these guys are good."

Cate loved the view of foothills building to mountains on the drive. She imagined herself climbing the peaks of every mountain and racing through the landscape on a horse with her hair blowing in the wind. The dirty brown snow of the city gave way to wide open snowy fields as they came closer to the mountains. "The skiing's supposed to be great, if you're interested," Gerald commented.

Cate had never been skiing. She doubted she should start now.

"Did I tell you, we'll be staying at the Banff Springs?" Robin turned to look at Cate in the back seat. She had mentioned it a number of times, but Cate didn't tell her. "We can go to the spa every day. They have these different pools with lovely names, I can't remember what they are, but three of them have waterfalls and you can soak inside this beautiful room with stone pillars or you can swim outside. At night, we can watch the stars."

"It sounds so fancy," Cate smiled.

"Robin loves fancy. You should see the room service she orders," Gerald teased.

Robin pretended to swat her husband's arm. "I'm so glad I'll have someone to appreciate these things with me," she said. "If it were up to my husband, all we'd do is eat burgers and watch sports highlights on a wide-screen T.V."

Gerald shrugged. "What could be better than that?" he replied.

They pulled past the park gates into Banff National Park. Cate gazed out the window admiringly. Every direction held a stunning view. They turned off the highway and drove past a large resort and then entered the town. Hotels, condos and restaurants were packed tightly on both sides of the street. They stopped at a restaurant called Giorgio's for lunch. "There's never any parking in this town," Gerald muttered before dropping them off.

"It's not the fanciest dining in Banff," Robin apologized. "But Gerald and I always come here. It was one of our first dates."

Cate gazed at the ice sculptures in front of the Italian eatery. She could see intimate, candle-lit tables through the windows and felt slightly uneasy. This restaurant was far more elegant than any she'd been to before. "Do you want to have lunch alone? I could go get something myself."

"You're not getting rid of us this early!" Robin latched onto Cate's arm. "You'll get time to explore on your own soon enough, but for now, you're still ours."

The awkwardness disappeared and Cate glowed with the feeling that she was wanted.

After Bruschetta, Calamari and Roseline, Cate was anxious for some fresh air. "Do you mind if I walk to the hotel? I'm so stuffed!" she said once the waiter came with a dish of olives.

Gerald waved her toward the door. "Yes, go, go. It's a beautiful day. Take your time."

Robin didn't look so sure, but she smiled and nodded at her guest. "Just ask for the Allens at the front desk. They'll tell you where to find us." She yawned and stretched. "I think I'm ready for a nap."

Gerald laughed. "This is what happens when you travel with an old couple."

Cate hugged him and blew a kiss at Robin. "You guys aren't old. I just need a bit of exercise."

The air was chilly outside of the restaurant, but it was a welcome relief. She headed in the direction of the hotel, but was forced to walk slowly to avoid the many tourists strolling along Banff Avenue. She trailed behind a family that included grandparents, aunts, uncles and two children in strollers. She couldn't take her eyes off the tourists to look around her because at any moment, they could stop dead in their tracks to pick up a bottle, a toy or just to stare at a window display.

After several of these stops, she dodged down Caribou Street, which was quieter and off the main drag. She followed the sidewalk, finally able to gaze at the mountains around her. She followed them until she came to the river.

"Beautiful," she breathed to herself, taking in the tall, snow-covered pines and the gurgling water that flowed between the ice. She breathed deeply and felt rejuvenated.

"It really is, isn't it," said a dark-haired young man sitting on a bench only a few metres away.

Cate blushed. "I didn't mean to talk to myself," she said.

He laughed and she noticed he held a sketch pad on his knee. He covered it quickly.

"I do it all the time," he said breezily. "I believe it's a sign of intelligence."

Cate snorted unexpectedly and blushed deeper. "Oh my."

He stood up and closed the distance between them. "A great compliment," he held out his hand. She was struck by his handsome features. "I'm Henry. Very nice to meet you."

"Cate," she murmured.

"One of my favourite names," he commented. "And where do you come from, Cate?"

She hoped the cool breeze off the water would take her blushes away. "I'm from Strathmore. East of Calgary."

"Hmm. I've never been there before. How do you like it?"

She wrinkled her nose. "Not much, but it's home."

"And this is mine," Henry gestured to include their surroundings.

"You mean, you live in Banff?" Cate pictured Henry living at the Banff Springs Hotel. Surely, he meant somewhere else, but she couldn't get the image out of her mind.

"That's right," he said and pointed down the river. "A few kilometres that way."

"Really? I didn't know anyone actually lived here."

Henry chuckled, his dark eyes crinkling. "You have no idea how many times I've heard that. So, what are your plans while you stay in town?"

Cate checked the time on her cellphone. She began to wonder if such a long conversation was appropriate with a stranger.

"I'm staying with my aunt and uncle at the Banff Springs," she lied, but felt it gave her some kind of protection to be travelling with family members.

She could tell Henry had noticed her discomfort. "Well then, maybe I'll run into you again," he said, gathering up his drawing instruments and returning to his previous activity. "Have a wonderful visit!"

Cate felt unsettled by the whole conversation, yet she hated to leave him so soon. It didn't help that she'd caught a glimpse of one of his very skilled drawings. "You too. I mean, have a good day." She tossed him a wave and hurried down the river path. She touched her cheek and found it was still quite hot.

CHAPTER FOUR

"Welcome!" Robin beamed with pleasure when Cate slid her key into the hotel room door.

A bellhop had insisted on seeing her to her room when she'd asked at the gingerbread-scented reception area. She'd been overcome by the huge entrance with its 20-foot Christmas tree and life-sized gingerbread house when she entered the hotel and was grateful for the young man who led her through the maze-like corridors.

Now, she gazed around the vaulted ceilings and arched windows. Robin gave the bellhop a tip and he disappeared from the doorway. Cate turned to look after him, reaching for her purse.

"Oh, I didn't even think. . ." she said, embarrassed.

Robin waved away her worries. "You're our guest. Let me show you your room."

Robin led her across the dark plush carpets to a door to her left. She opened it with a flourish. The first thing Cate noticed was the perfectly centred chandelier over a gold and cream bedspread. She walked in slowly, holding her breath.

"I really don't need all this," she said, taking in the fireplace in the corner of her room and the window seat nestled into a bay window.

Robin put a hand on her shoulder. "What is it worth if you can't share it?" she said. "I'll give you a few minutes to settle in and then, I was hoping we could visit the spa, if you aren't too tired. I made a booking for massages at 4:00. Gerald hates getting massages, he thinks they aren't manly or something. I can't wait to go with someone who appreciates nice things."

Cate smiled. "That sounds wonderful. Thank you."

Robin exited the room, closing the door noiselessly behind her. Cate was so relieved she had new luggage for her trip. She imagined bringing her dented blue suitcase with the broken handle into this pristine room and shuddered at the idea. She drifted over to her new cases and began unpacking them into the mahogany armoire her room provided.

When her new clothes were neatly put away, she allowed herself to sit in the brocade-padded window seat. She looked out over a raging waterfall cutting into the rocky landscape. Mountains rose out of the river and to her right was a snow-covered golf course which seemed to be set with some kind of track. Busloads of visitors unloaded to gaze at the scenery while she watched from the comfort of her spacious bedroom. She smiled contentedly.

After checking into the eucalyptus-scented spa reception area, Robin and Cate were led to an elegant locker room where they changed into robes. "You can put your swimsuit on after the massage. It is so nice to soak in the warm water when you're done and I think it makes the massage last longer."

Cate wasn't sure about being naked under her robe. She kept her underwear on, though she noticed Robin did not.

"Let's go have something to drink," she said once their thick robes were secured. She led them through a labyrinth of hallways to a comfortable sitting room. A small refrigerator boasted several types of water and other colourful drinks, there was also a coffee machine with an abundance of hot beverage selections. A basket of fruit and a tray of cookies were centred on a table between the flowery couches and armchairs.

"What would you like?" Robin gestured to the selection. "Help yourself." She chose a coffee cup and slipped it into the coffee machine while Cate chose a sparkling lemonade. Two other women sat drinking tea and leafing through fashion magazines. Cate judged them to be mother and daughter by the similar blond hair, facial features and the age difference. The younger woman looked about her age.

They sat a few chairs down from them until the older woman looked up.

"Robin Allen. Is that you?" the older woman stood up to gain a closer look.

"Sarah Thorpe! Well if that isn't the nicest surprise." The two women hugged and Cate noticed the daughter looking up from her magazine.

"What has it been, 20 years?" Sarah asked.

Robin laughed. "I don't think I want to admit how many years."

"And is this your daughter?" Sarah motioned to Cate.

"No, no. We never did have children. My niece, of sorts," Robin winked at Cate. "This is Cate Morland."

Sarah shook her hand and motioned to the other woman. "This is my daughter, Isabella. She's eighteen. How about you?"

"Mother, really." Isabella said, rolling her eyes. She stood up and shook first Robin's and then Cate's hand. "Nice to meet you," she said. She had an infectious smile and small, straight white teeth.

"I'm eighteen as well," replied Cate. She and Robin joined the two women. Robin and Sarah began remembering their high school days in Strathmore, but after a story or two, Isabella seemed to grow impatient with their talk.

"So, how long will you be staying at the Springs?" she motioned to the hotel with her French-manicured hands.

"Five days," Cate said, shyly. Isabella seemed much more sophisticated than she was.

"Then you'll be here for the ball," she said, her eyes sparkling. "They have one every Christmas. Have you been before? I don't remember seeing you." She scrunched her brow prettily, as if trying to recall.

"No, never. What happens at the ball?" Cate took a small sip of her lemonade, the bubbles fizzing in her nose, making her sneeze.

"Bless you. Well, it's really old-fashioned. Everyone dresses up and there are dance cards for the girls. The guys have to ask you for a dance and you write their names by the numbers. Once you fill in all the places, your dance card is full and you have to turn the rest of the boys down." Isabella shrugged her shoulders and lifted her eyebrows playfully. "I had my card full by 9 p.m. last year. I'm hoping to fill it before 8:30, this year. It's kind of like a contest."

"Oh?" Cate thought it sounded awful. What if no one asked her to dance and her dance card gaped open all night?

"What kind of dress do you have?" Isabella asked.

"Well, I hadn't thought to bring one. . ."

Isabella shook her head. "That won't do, you'll have to go shopping immediately."

Cate smiled then, remember what Robin had told her when they looked through her new luggage at her house. "Wait, I do have a dress," she smiled. "Robin bought one for me, I just remembered. I haven't seen it yet."

Isabella rolled her eyes and spoke lowly. "If I were you, I'd make sure I saw the dress ahead of time. You never know what these old ladies will think is in," she jerked a thumb toward her mother. "You might have enough time to find something in town, but you'd think all anybody wore here was Banff t-shirts and winter parkas from what they offer in their stores." She pulled a disapproving face and sipped her tea.

"What kind of dress will you be wearing?" Cate asked.

Isabella's eyes lit up. "Oh, it's divine. I was totally inspired by one of the dresses at the Golden Globes, you know the red one?"

Cate didn't really, but she nodded her head.

"So I went online to find out where I could get the dress and I totally found it. My mom, of course, didn't want to order online, but I used my magic and voila, I got the dress! It looks almost as good on me as it did on T.V. I think I have better lips, but that actress's eyes are sooo unusual." Isabella seemed to be waiting for Cate to say something.

"You have lovely eyes," she said, more like a question than a statement.

"Well, one of the guys at my school once told me they were like pools of ice," she said with false modesty.

Cate couldn't quite figure out if that was a good thing or not, but she smiled anyway.

A woman dressed in a white uniform entered the room on soft shoes. "Mrs. Thorpe, Ms. Thorpe," she said melodically. "Your therapist is ready."

"Finally," Isabella mock-whispered.

"We'll see you at dinner then," Sarah waved her fingers at them. "It's been a real pleasure," she nodded at Cate. Then the women disappeared down the hallway and Cate felt like she could breathe again.

"You seemed to get along well," Robin said. "I hope you don't mind that I called you my niece." She squeezed Cate's hand. "I just feel like I'm the only woman without a child, sometimes."

"Of course you can call me your niece," Cate squeezed back. "Aunty Robin," she teased.

Robin grinned.

The massage felt wonderful. Cate chose to have hot rocks and they relaxed knots she never knew she had in her shoulders. The massage therapist didn't mention her underwear and Cate chose grapefruit aromatherapy to invigorate her senses.

They returned to the dressing room and Cate was pleased to find that the 2-piece swimsuit Robin bought her fit perfectly.

"So pretty!" remarked Robin.

"How did you get all the right sizes for me?" she asked while admiring the sparkly blue suit in the mirror.

"Oh, that," Robin waved a hand dismissively. "I used to work in a ladies clothing store before I met Gerald. I just had a knack for knowing women's sizes."

"But a swimsuit is really hard to fit," Cate said.

Robin spoke conspiratorially. "It's all about being honest. I found that I had a better perspective of other women's bodies than they had. They'd tell me their sizes and I'd bring them the size they really were. Sometimes they'd notice and yell at me, but I'd just say 'Oh sorry, I must have grabbed the wrong one.' But most of the time, they wouldn't notice and they'd be so thrilled that something looked so good on them."

Cate took another look at the back of her suit. "Well, you certainly have me pegged. You can shop for me anytime."

They stepped out of the dressing room into the pool room. The glass ceiling rose high above them, supported by tall marble columns. The sound of falling water filled the space from the three separate waterfall pools. The room was surrounded by windows overlooking an outdoor pool, tall pine trees and those majestic mountains.

"It's wonderful," Cate breathed.

Robin squeezed her shoulder. "I'm so glad you like it. I love this room. Where do you want to start?"

Cate gazed at the four pools and pointed at the waterfall closest to them. "How's that?" she asked.

"Perfect," Robin said and they sunk into the steaming, roiling water. They both sighed and then laughed at themselves.

"I don't know if you overheard much of my conversation with Sarah," Robin said through closed eyes.

"A bit," Cate replied.

"Apparently Isabella's brother is good friends with your brother," she opened her eyes to smile at Cate.

"Really? Isabella never mentioned anything."

"It took a bit of sleuthing," Robin said. "Sarah thought your last name sounded familiar and after thinking it over, she realized James attends the same University as her son, John. They're both studying engineering and, in fact, James and John are driving up this afternoon to spend the weekend with the Thorpes."

"James is coming here?" Cate's eyes snapped open. "Why didn't he tell me?"

"I guess it was a last minute decision," Robin looked delighted. "We'll be having dinner with them tonight."

Cate hugged her friend. "Oh, that's perfect. I can't wait to see him. It's like this was all meant to happen." Cate gestured around the hotel.

Robin chortled. "Yes it is. It's like magic."

CHAPTER FIVE

The Allens and Cate met the Thorpes and her brother in a large dining room called the Bow Valley Grill at the hotel which overlooked a skating rink. The mountains rose like soldiers guarding the castle, the river nestled between the two.

"James! I'm so glad to see you again." Cate ran up to her brother and hugged him. They had always been close – the closest in age among the five siblings and the closest in temperament.

"Hey Catherine," her brother chuckled. "Long time no see." He gave her a bear hug. "Don't you look nice," he said, holding her back from him. "This is my friend John."

James clapped his friend on the back and John stuck out his hand to Cate.

"Gorgeous," John appraised her and Cate blushed. "You never told me your sister was so hot."

James place a protective arm around her shoulder. "Not cool, man," he said. "That's my little sister you're talking about." But he gave his friend a wink.

"These boys," Isabella claimed Cate's arm. "It's like they were raised by monkeys." She patted James' arm and Cate noticed a certain look between the pair.

"The waiter's ready for us," Gerald interrupted them. "I'm starved."

They sat at a large old-fashioned oak table with high-backed chairs. "It's like a fairy tale," Cate breathed.

Isabella giggled. "Minus the princes on white horses," she teased.

"Hey, I'll have you know, I've ridden horses before," John boasted. "There just didn't happen to be any white ones."

"If you want horses, I heard you can book sleigh rides that leave right from the hotel," James sounded eager to please Isabella.

"That sounds fun!" Isabella chirped and her softly curled blond hair bounced around her bare shoulders. She was wearing a skimpy black dress that made Cate a little embarrassed.

"What do you say, Cate?" John turned to her, his eyes playful. "Would you like to go galloping through the forest with us?"

Cate worried about the money, but she hoped she had enough. "Okay. I've never been on a sleigh ride before. Do they tell you what to do first?"

John laughed and patted her hand. "You'll be just fine. I promise we'll take good care of you."

The waiter arrived to take their drink orders. Then Sarah Thorpe began asking Cate a lot of questions about Strathmore and what she was taking at school. She managed to order the halibut and was delighted by the unusual pairing of red cabbage kimchi and turnips.

"I've never had this before," she murmured when her plate arrived.

"James, your sister is the cutest girl I've ever met," John said, gazing at her with his chin in his hand.

Cate looked nervously around the table. She'd never met someone who said thing like he did, in front of his mother, no less. Not to mention, this was the first time they'd met. She caught Robin looking at her with an air of concern, but the conversation continued and Cate was relieved when John became involved in a complicated discussion with her brother about the ethics of engineering.

"I don't supposed you've heard the ghost stories of the hotel?" John said once their after-dinner coffees arrived. He had ordered rum.

A shiver ran across Cate's neck. Of course, a castle must have a ghost story! She leaned a little closer to hear.

"You'll notice a stair case through there," John pointed toward the opposite side of the restaurant. There were two decorative doors with glass windows which Cate hadn't noticed before.

"I love ghost stories!" Isabella clutched James' bicep. He smiled at her and patted her small white hand.

"I heard from one of the chambermaids that there was a wedding here, 100 years ago or so, and a bride stood at the top of the stairs, waiting to meet her new husband. Just as she started to descend, she tripped and fell head first down the stairs. She broke her neck and died instantly, without ever enjoying her wedding night," he winked at Cate. She realized she'd been staring at him as he told the story and looked away quickly.

"Some say it was her jealous maid who pushed her just before. She later married the husband and his dead bride now searches the hotel for her groom. The chambermaid told me she could hear the bride tapping on the doors or moaning through the old pipes when she's cleaning alone. She told me guests have complained about seeing a bride through a window in the west wing."

The hairs on Cate's arms stood on end. She took a sip of her coffee, trying to ward off her shivers.

"That's terrible," she breathed. "To go to all that work and never get married."

"The staircase was blocked off for years. The hotel manager worried someone else would fall down the slick marble, but in a recent renovation, it was reopened. They say you can still make out a faint blood stain."

"Let's go see it!" Isabella clapped her hands excitedly.

James hurried to stand and pull out Isabella's chair. John cocked an eyebrow at Cate and she couldn't dismiss her curiosity.

"We'll be right back," John squeezed his mother's shoulder and then took Cate's hand and placed it in the crook of his arm. "Right this way," he said and the foursome wound through the tables toward the back door.

"Going to visit the ghost?" a pretty waitress holding a tray full of drinks smiled at them.

"Have you seen her?" Cate couldn't help asking.

The waitress shook her long, dark hair. "Seen her, no. But I once felt her when I was alone in the dining room. There were hardly any customers and I was the only one serving. The power flickered out for a few minutes and I felt an icy hand on my arm." She shivered daintily. "Boy was I glad when the lights came back on."

"Creepy!" squealed Isabella.

They continued through the door and took in the spiralling stone staircase with dark winding banisters. "It doesn't look that steep," said John.

"Where's the stain?" asked Isabella. The small room below the staircase was furnished with several armchairs and a chaise longue. There were pictures on the walls of meadows and mountains. The space was lit by wall sconces which projected shadows around the area.

The party spread out in search of discoloration. There were several places in the old marble that looked darker. They guessed at a few places near the bottom step, but no one could be sure. "It's so sad," Cate said to her brother. They gave up the hunt then and returned to the table to find the Allens and Thorpes had taken care of the bill.

"What's your room number?" Isabella asked her as they collected their purses.

"417," she said.

"We'll call you in the morning to arrange the sleigh ride," she kissed Cate's cheek. "Hope you don't hear any ghosts in your sleep," she giggled.

"You too!" she replied.

Cate awoke to a tapping at her door. She sat up with a jolt in her queen-sized bed. Her clock read 3:13. She hurried to switch on her bedside lamp, but the bulb popped as soon as she pulled the cord. She tried to remember the layout of her room as she recalled she was not at home and padded toward the sound of the knocking. When she opened her door, there was no one there. She could hear Gerald snoring in the darkness and was about to call out, but stopped herself. She didn't want to disturb her kind hosts. She must have been dreaming. She returned to her bed and sank into the still-warm sheets, but her heart was racing.

When she closed her eyes, she continually saw an old-fashioned bride tumbling down the curved marble staircase. She tried rolling from one side to the other, lying on her back and her stomach, but the vision would not go away. Then she heard the knocking again and a whisper breathed onto her cheek. But when she tried to get up, she discovered she was sleeping. The process repeated itself again and again. She could never tell if she was awake or asleep. At one point, she thought she heard the words "Too late," in her ear and felt a hand on her cheek, but she could not scream.

CHAPTER SIX

"Cate!" Robin's familiar sing-song voice whispered through her tall oak door. "Are you awake?"

Cate pushed herself to sit up and found her bedding in complete disarray. "I'm here!" she called, relieved to see some light coming through her thick curtains. When she pulled on her bedside light, she shook her head at the memory of her fretful night.

"I'm ordering room service," Robin peeked her head through the door. "Oh my! Were you wrestling a bear last night?" her laughter tinkled through the room, chasing away ghosts and other worries.

"I'm not sure." she scratched her head and felt how tangled her hair was. "I think I was having a nightmare."

"Poor girl," Robin sat down beside her and felt her forehead with the back of her hand. "You look quite red. But no fever."

Cate forced herself to laugh. "I had no idea I was such a sucker for a ghost story."

Robin removed her hand. "I was about to order breakfast. Are you hungry yet?"

"Starving!" she replied. "I guess I worked up an appetite."

Robin produced a breakfast menu from her robe. "I'm having the Eggs Benedict. What would you like?"

Cate tried not to gasp at the prices. "Just some toast," she said, although she could have bought an entire breakfast for her family for the price.

Robin looked at her closely. "Please don't worry about the cost. I'll order a few extra things. Toast doesn't cure starving and I think you'll need more than bread to get over your night. I'll let you know when it comes."

Robin padded out of the room and Cate lay back in her pillows. It was an overwhelming way to wake up and she needed a few minutes and a shower before she could stop shaking.

"Are you sure you won't come skiing with us?" Gerald asked after they'd eaten an enormous breakfast and read through the newspaper.

"I promised the Thorpe's I'd go on a sleigh ride today," Cate said apologetically.

"When are they going?" Robin asked, taking a sip from her tea.

Cate wrinkled her forehead. "I'm not really sure," she said.

"Seems a waste to wait around for them all day. I think most sleigh rides happen at night," Gerald said, but just then their hotel phone rang.

"Good morning!" Isabella said through the connection. "How did you sleep?"

"Not well," Cate admitted.

"Oh dear," Isabella sounded delighted. "You'll have to tell me all about it. Well, we've booked the ride for 11 o'clock. Can you come?"

"Sure," Cate said. "Where should we meet?"

"We'll pick you up. Don't worry about a thing. Maybe I'll come a bit early so I can tell you what happened to me last night," Isabella giggled.

Cate felt a rush of concern that her brother was somehow involved.

"So James and John shared the extra room last night," Isabella said as she leafed through the outfits in Cate's closet. "And wouldn't you know, I had a knock on my door at midnight." She studied Cate's evening dress. "I don't know. Do you think this is enough?" she lifted the flowing material to get a closer look. "Don't you want to stand out a bit more?"

She held the dress up to her own body and Cate considered how much more it covered than the dress her friend had worn to dinner last night.

"Robin bought it for me," Cate said, loyally. "I think it's perfect."

Isabella shrugged her shoulders and returned the garment to the closet, closing the door with a flourish. "So, anyway, he wanted to go for a walk to the Bow Falls. Mom was already asleep, so I didn't bother asking. I was already in my cute little teddy, so I asked him to come in while I put on something a little warmer, but your brother is a real gentleman."

Cate tried not to grimace. She really didn't want to know any more of her brother's romantic exploits. Especially with Isabella, she realized, though she wasn't sure why.

"So then he took me to the Bow Falls," Isabella continue while gazing at herself in the mirror. She pursed her lips in the style of a fashion model and petted her long, straight blond hair. "It was sooo romantic," she said. "And then he kissed me." She sighed and smiled at herself in the mirror.

"Well, that's very nice." Cate murmured.

"Aren't you the little prude," Isabella teased. "You won't be for long if my brother has anything to do with it," she winked. "He has plans for you."

Before Cate could ask more, there was a knock at the door and she found her brother and John waiting behind it. "All ready girls?" John asked with a smile that seemed to know too much. He took her hand proprietorially and expertly led the foursome through the carpeted hallways.

"I think this will do nicely for some after-sleighing drinks." John pointed out a high-ceiling room with two fireplaces, several velvet-red couches, a large Christmas tree and a conveniently placed bar. "They don't open until 4, but I think we can wait that long."

Cate smiled meekly at him in response. She felt like he was a million miles ahead of her and she was just trying to keep up.

The walked through an octagonal room with windows along every side and then out to a driveway she had not seen before. There were two large horses waiting with an old-fashioned wooden sleigh. It was just big enough for the four of them.

"After you," John pointed toward the contraption and Cate took the two steps up into a fur-lined seat.

"There you are," the driver said enthusiastically.

Cate looked up and recognized Henry. 'Oh!" she said, surprised. "I didn't know you'd be here."

"Isn't that nice," John said with a muted sneer. "You know the help."

"Henry Tilney," he held out his hand to John, ignoring the snub. "I'll be your driver this morning."

"Tilney?" Isabella disentangled herself from her intimate conversation with James. "Are you related to General Tilney?" Her voice had an excited lilt to it.

"My father," Henry nodded. "Do you know him?"

Isabella squealed. "I wish. You must be as rich as Texas. Why do you have to drive the horses? Shouldn't you be living the life of luxury?"

Henry stepped down from his perch to adjust a strap on one of the animals. "My Dad doesn't believe in being lazy or spoiled. He's had me working at the hotel since I can remember. Whatever job he can't fill, he passes on to me or my sister."

"You have a sister?" Cate asked.

"Yes," Henry turned to smile at her. "Eleanor. I call her Ellie. Eleanor is such an old-fashioned name. Henry too, I guess, but it doesn't shorten to anything much. You should meet her. I think you'd get along."

"Maybe she's cleaning our room right now," Isabella tittered. "Imagine, the son of the General Tilney leading our sleigh ride. Mom will never believe me."

Henry handed out blankets and made sure they were comfortable.

"We'll be heading down past the golf course, if that's okay. I have you booked until 3 p.m., right?"

"You bet," John said with a clipped edge to his voice. He didn't seem to like all the attention Henry was getting.

"I'll let you out about halfway through for a picnic at the clubhouse. It isn't fully staffed this time of the year, but I think you'll enjoy the lunch they offer."

John waved his hand around in the air. "Let's go, already," he said, rudely.

"Of course," Henry turned forward and urged the horses on.

John put his arm around Cate's shoulders. She tried to lean away from him and his assumptions, but the seat was tight and she had nowhere else to go.

Henry guided the horses around a steep set of switchbacks. John complained about the slowness of the ride, but the rest of them ignored him.

"I can't believe our luck!" Isabella leaned toward Cate conspiratorially. "How is Henry Tilney our driver? I'll have to be careful how we treat all of the employees at the hotel. How do you know him, Cate?"

"I met him in town," Cate said.

"Is that all?" her brother interrupted. "He seemed to know you better than that."

"That's all," Cate glanced at John's furrowed brow.

"We should have gone skiing instead." John seemed agitated. "I think this is going to be boring. If it weren't for you girls talking about princes on horses. . . I bet you think this Henry Tilney is quite the catch."

Cate was alarmed at John's jealousy. She wasn't even his girlfriend.

CHAPTER SEVEN

Henry pointed out the waterfall, the names of the mountains and shared a bit of history when there was a lull in the conversation, but he never looked behind him and John seemed to relax from his initial misgivings.

"So, what are you planning to wear to the party tonight?" he said with a rather lascivious gaze at Cate.

"You'll hate it," Isabella answered for her. "I don't think you'll see any cleavage at all. Her aunt picked it out."

"Aunt?" James said.

"You know, Robin," Isabella shook her head at him and then planted a kiss on his cheek. "Silly men."

"I'm only allowed to fill in two of your dance card spots," John said to Cate, running a finger along her arm. "But I have several code names I can use."

Cate tried to squirm away from him. "Why can you only fill in two spots?" Cate asked, although she mentally kicked herself. She didn't want to encourage him.

John rolled his eyes. "Some archaic rule. The Tilneys came up with the idea for this ball. I think it was the sister who is obsessed with England and princesses and all that garbage. She must have seen it in a movie or something. There are all kinds of rules. I think the chicks like it. You can only do old-school dances, no kissing or hand holding or anything. If it weren't for the girls in hot dresses, no guy would be caught dead at the thing, but what can you do?" John opened his hands expansively. "Gotta keep you girls happy."

Cate was relieved when the sleigh slowed as it approached a teepee-shaped building nestled between the mountains. The clubhouse was generously sprinkled with windows and she looked forward to the view, hopefully away from John's reach.

Henry stopped the horses at a hitching post and jumped down from his seat. "Just hold on one moment while I get them settled," he called.

"Forget that," John replied under his breath and began standing up. One of the horses jerked suddenly and John lost his balance. His arms flailed around and Cate reached out to steady him. She couldn't help giggling. He managed not to topple over, but he retook his seat until Henry came around to help them out of the sleigh.

"Right this way," he directed them.

Sun sparkled on the snow-covered golf-course. Henry led the group into the clubhouse.

A young woman with short-cropped blond hair met them at the door wearing a hotel uniform.

"Hey Ellie," Henry greeted her with a kiss on the cheek. "I didn't know you'd be here today."

"You just never know where you'll end up when you're a Tilney at the Banff Springs Hotel," she said with a smile, but her eyes looked sad. "I'm Eleanor Tilney, Ellie." She held out her hand to Cate.

"Cate Morland," she shook her hand warmly. "I know your brother. Well, a little. This is my brother, James," she pointed to him. He shook her hand as well and then she introduced Isabella and, lastly, John.

"I'm so glad you could come," Ellie said.

"Two Tilenys in one day," Isabella said. "I just can't get over that you are working at the hotel. And for us, no less!"

"We're just like anybody else," Ellie said quietly. "Come right this way," she said in a more businesslike tone. She brought them into an open, window-lined room where a heavy picnic-blanket was spread out in front of a crackling fireplace. Of course, the blanket was surrounded by comfortable leather sofas, but it offered an imagined picnic.

"There's tea and hot chocolate in the pots," Ellie motioned to two silver teapots and some white china cups. "I believe you ordered the sandwich and fruit trays," she consulted a black leather booklet.

"That's right," John sniffed.

"Is there anything else you'd like to add?" Ellie asked.

"No, thank you." John replied.

Cate was suspicious of John's disinterest in their server. He had certainly seemed interested in every other woman she'd seen him with. Perhaps he was still sore about tripping in the sleigh.

James stretched out on the picnic blanket and soon Isabella joined him. They spoke in low voices which were obviously meant to contain a private conversation. John seemed to be eying the empty spot Isabella left beside Cate on the sofa.

"I'll be right back," she stood up before he could make a move. She exited the room, pretending to search for the ladies room. She bumped into Ellie on the way.

"Oh, hello. Where is the. . ."

"Right this way," Ellie pointed to a sign.

Cate stalled. "Thank you so much for arranging our lunch," she said awkwardly.

"Oh, it's no trouble. Happy to help." Ellie smoothed a strip of hair across her brow.

"I met your brother by the river," she explained. "He was drawing. Is he an artist?"

This was the right question. "Oh yes. He's very talented. He's studying art at a college in Calgary. Well, he was accepted at several better schools, but since our mother died, he hates to be too far away."

"I'm so sorry," Cate's hand went to her mouth. "I didn't know."

The sadness returned to Ellie's eyes. "Thank you," she said softly. "Are you going to the ball tonight?" she said a moment later.

"Yes," Cate said. "I hear it's incredible."

Ellie grinned. "I'm glad. It's kind of a pet project of mine. I need to go collect some things in the kitchen, but maybe we can talk more tonight." She squeezed Cate's shoulder and Cate felt the warmth of possible friendship through her arm.

John remained taciturn for the remainder of the meal. Cate thought she must have offended him when she accidently giggled at him, but felt no compunction to alleviate the problem. She didn't want to lead him on.

The sandwiches and fruit were delicious and Cate couldn't keep herself from drinking several cups of hot chocolate. Then Henry collected them back into the sleigh and John made no move to put his arm around her. James and Isabella, on the other hand, sat even closer together and stole kisses all the way back to the hotel. Cate tried to look away.

CHAPTER EIGHT

When they arrived back at the hotel, she reached into her purse to pay for her portion of the adventure. "How much do I owe?" she asked James. She was too embarrassed to ask John or Isabella.

"Don't worry sis," James said. "The Allens covered the whole thing."

"Oh no," Cate brought her hand to her mouth. "Mom didn't want me to take advantage of their generosity."

Her brother gave her a one-armed hug. "Don't worry about Mom. She doesn't need to know everything."

Cate wished she and her brother could escape from the Thorpes for a while, but he seemed to have no such desire.

"How about a swim?" he suggested.

"I should spend some time with the Allens this afternoon. Thank you for the sleigh ride," she said to Isabella and John.

"I'll come to your room to help you get ready tonight," Isabella hugged her. "I can't wait!"

"Cate! I'm so glad you're back," Robin greeted her in the hotel room. "How was your ride?"

"Wonderful," Cate forced a smile. She didn't want to appear ungrateful.

"Oh, to be young again," she sighed. "I left Gerald up at the hill. I was so cold and he just wanted to ski and ski." She waved her hands around, as if to imitate a skiing motion. "Well, I think we have time for another trip to the spa before dinner. Are you up for it?"

The cost of her stay to the Allens piled up in Cate's mind, but she couldn't disappoint her hostess, especially when she'd been away all morning.

"I'll go get my suit," she promised.

Cate and the Allens had dinner in the Rundle Lounge where Gerald enjoyed several Hot Toddies and relived his day on the hill.

"You have to come with us next time, Cate. The wind in your hair as you rush down the hill. . . There's nothing like it!" His cheeks were red and his voice louder than usual.

Cate continually scanned the room, but so far, no Thorpes had turned up.

"There's a lovely tradition at the hotel on Christmas Eve before the ball," Robin said, taking a dainty bite of her Coriander and Lemongrass Seared Tuna Salad. "The owner of the hotel and his family lead some Christmas carols in Mount Stephen Hall. Would you like to go to that?"

Cate perked up at the thought of seeing Ellie and Henry again. "That sounds perfect. But I think I might call home first, it that's okay."

"Of course!" Robin froze. "I'm only sorry I didn't think of that. You must be missing your mom and brothers terribly." She looked at Cate's nearly empty plate. "You can go right now, if you like. I hope your Mom doesn't mind too much that we've taken you away." She looked concerned.

Cate tried to give an encouraging smile. "I'm sure they're fine. I just don't want to forget. Thank you for dinner."

She rose and folded her linen napkin neatly beside her plate. "I'll just be in our room."

"Merry Christmas sweetheart," Cate's mom sounded like she was holding back tears.

"What are you and the boys doing tonight?" Cate asked, trying to make her voice sound as cheerful as possible in the hopes of raising her mother's spirits.

"We'll be going to the Neufeld's tonight," Cate's mother seemed to collect herself. "Hot chocolate and sledding and I'm sure lots of treats. I made shortbread with the boys today, but of course they lost interest half way through, so I mostly did it myself."

Cate felt a pang of home-sickness. Usually she helped her mom with the Christmas baking, but then she thought of the upcoming ball and it went away.

"I've met a few people here at the hotel," Cate said. "James' friends, but also the owner's family."

"The owner of what, honey?" her mother asked. It sounded like she was wiping her nose with a tissue.

"The hotel!" Cate said. "They're very ordinary people. Well, his son and daughter anyway. I haven't actually met Mr. Tilney, but his son Henry and daughter Ellie work at the hotel."

"I suppose they have to learn the business somehow," her mother mumbled. "Are they nice?"

"Yes, very. I think we'll see them tonight at the ball and carol-singing." Cate hoped she didn't sound like she was trying to show off.

Her mother sighed. "Sounds like a fairy tale. Just remember where you come from, Cate. You're going to have to leave there and come back to real life, you know."

Cate shook her head, even though she knew her mother couldn't see her. "I know, Mom. But it's a nice vacation. Wish you were here."

"I miss you," her mom sounded wistful.

They ended the call shortly after and then the Allens returned.

"How was Amy?" Gerald asked, slumping into one of the room's comfortable sofas.

"Fine," Cate smiled. "She misses me."

Robin came over to hug her. "I hope she doesn't mind too much. It's so nice to have a 'niece' for the holidays."

"She'll be okay," Cate said. "She has all my brothers and they're going to the Neufeld's tonight."

"I'm glad," Robin smoothed a strand of Cate's hair. "I think it's time we got ready. The singing starts in about 45 minutes. Do you need help?" she looked hopeful.

"I might," Cate said. "I'll let you know."

She skipped to her room and closed the door behind her.

CHAPTER NINE

Mount Stephen Hall looked exactly the way a castle hall should look. It was a long room with wooden beams overhead, tall arched windows and a polished marble floor. A large gingerbread house marked the entrance to the hall. It was made to look like the Banff Springs Hotel with Mini-Wheats for shingles, candied fruit windows, and white fondant snowmen.

"I once tried to pull a candy to eat from this house," Isabella came up behind Cate and whispered in her ear. "But it was stuck on too tightly and I couldn't break it off."

Cate whirled around to find her friend adorned in a very tight and revealing red dress. Her long hair was straightened with military precision. She spun around with her hands above her head. "What do you think?"

"You look very nice," Cate said.

Isabella lips curled as if she'd eaten something sour. "Nice wasn't really what I was going for. You look divine!"

Cate looked down at her long blue gown. It seemed to float around the floor with light, airy fabric. A long silver tassel wound around her body from her feet up to her left shoulder. It was certainly more modest than her friend's, but she thought it was much finer. She touched her hair lightly, remembering the way Robin had styled it into a loose shiny roll and couldn't help hoping Henry would see her.

"Thank you," she replied.

The Thorpes joined the Allens in a long row of chairs halfway from the front. Seats were filling quickly and she was glad they'd arrived early. A huge Christmas tree rose from floor to ceiling in front of the tall window at the front of the room. Chandeliers hung overhead and pine wreaths hung from the columns. The tree and wreaths were decorated with rich red bows and white Christmas lights sparkled around the room.

"It must take forever to decorate," Robin mused.

John and James arrived just before the pianist and John took the empty seat to Cate's left. She had hoped her brother would sit beside her, but he headed directly to Isabella's side.

"You look delicious," John whispered in her ear once he'd greeted the rest of the group. "Don't forget to give me the first look at your dance card." But he wasn't eying her dance card.

Cate felt a shiver up her neck.

"You know, I think I saw the bellhop this afternoon," he said, gazing around the room.

"What bellhop?" Cate asked.

John grinned. "Another of this hotel's deep, dark secrets." He wiggled his eyebrows at her. The others in their party were involved in their own conversations.

"Well, tell me," Cate said when John's pause went on.

"Sam was an immigrant from Scotland who worked at the hotel for many years. Apparently he loved the hotel and wanted to die working here, but the management forced him to retire in 1978. He died that very night, without even receiving his last paycheck."

"So does he go around, searching for money?" Cate clutched her small purse closer and tried to ignore the hair raising on her arms.

"No, he's a friendly, helpful ghost. He carries people's luggage and lets them into their rooms when they get locked out."

Cate felt some relief at this response. "Where did you see him?"

"Well, I was looking for room 873. There is no room 873. There's an 872 and an 874, but 873 has been blocked forever."

"Why?" Cate asked, chills ran up her neck this time.

"They say a family was murdered inside and even though they cleaned the room, they could never get the little girl's fingerprints off of the mirror."

Cate shuddered, but John could not continue terrifying her because just then, a pianist began to play "Angels We Have Heard on High" on the large grand piano. Cate reached for the booklet of songs she'd been given and opened to the correct page. John reached for the left side of the booklet to share it with her.

There was also a cello and violin to accompany the piano. The voices and instruments rose magnificently into the rafters and would have been beautiful if John's toneless singing hadn't overwhelmed all that Cate could hear. He seemed to be trying to make up for his lack of musicality by singing louder. Cate let her voice sink to a whisper. No amount of leaning away from her chair mate could diminish the sound.

Cate resigned herself to an hour or two of continued awfulness and was plotting her escape to the ladies room when the musicians stood up and moved away from the stage. Had John's voice carried all the way up to them? Then she saw Henry and Ellie approaching from one of the stone archways. They were led by a tall burly man with a salt and pepper beard, wearing a tuxedo. When they gained the front of the hall, the man bellowed loudly enough for all of the assemble guest to hear him without a microphone.

"Merry Christmas to all of our honoured guests," he began with a hint of a Scottish brogue. For some reason, his voice and appearance filled Cate with gloom. "I am General Tilney, owner of the Banff Springs Hotel."

A round of applause greeted this announcement. He waited with a stern expression until the clapping died away. "My children have prepared a special musical piece for you tonight. Henry is at the piano and Eleanor will be singing. Enjoy."

He bowed smartly and disappeared into the crowd as Henry began to play with the skill of a professional.

"Oh holy night, the stars are brightly shining. . ." Ellie's voice was high and sweet.

Cate noticed that John sat up higher in the seat before him and willed him not to hum along. Fortunately, he didn't.

Henry sang harmony sparingly during the performance. Cate could feel her heart quicken as they sang and a contented smile softened her features. The song ended before Cate was ready for it to be over. There was a brief, awed silence in the hall before the crowd rose to give the Tilneys a standing ovation. Despite calls for an encore, the original pianist and his fellow players retook the instruments and the crowd remained on its feet to singing Jingle Bells, Walking in a Winter Wonderland and finally, Silent Night. The Tilneys joined the musicians to sing the final song, but Cate couldn't hear them over John.

Cate attempted to make her way to the front to congratulate her friends, but the hall was crowded and she was trapped in conversation first with John and then with Isabella.

"Isn't this the coziest way to spend Christmas Eve!" she trilled. "I had no idea the Tilneys were so talented." She seemed to make this last statement with a sneer. Cate wondered briefly if her friend sang as badly as her brother. Perhaps the family did not have much appreciation for music.

"Well, we haven't a minute to lose," Isabella said once the room began to clear. "The ball will be starting shortly and we have our dance cards to fill."

Cate yawned and wondered if she had the energy for a ball yet. It had been a very full day.

CHAPTER TEN

Isabella insisted Cate come back to her room to freshen up for the gala. Her accommodations were smaller and less elaborate than the Allens'. There was a separate bedroom shared by James and John while Isabella and Mrs. Thorpe shared the main area. Their bathroom was strewn with a multitude of beauty products.

"Come in here," Isabella motioned and then locked them into the cramped room together.

"Your brother is so sexy," Isabella sighed and pulled out a tube of mascara.

Cate cringed.

"I really think tonight might be the night!" she applied another coat of plumping product to her already caked eyelashes.

Cate tried to smooth a few stray chestnut hairs. She didn't want to know what 'the night' meant to Isabella, but she had a pretty good idea and wondered how the sleeping arrangements in their small hotel room would allow for such an occasion.

"You and my brother are sure getting cozy," she elbowed Cate softly.

Cate frowned into the mirror. "I really don't think so," she replied. "We were just sitting next to one another. I'm really more interested in. . ."

Isabella interrupted through her newest layer of lip gloss. "You two will look absolutely divine on the dance floor. I'm sure no one will notice little old me, but maybe your handsome brother will draw some attention." Isabella pouted at her reflection, as if waiting for Cate's response.

Cate suppressed a giggle. She loved and admired her eldest brother, but no one, she was sure, had ever considered him good looking. "I'm sure you'll stand out on the dance floor," she soothed. "That dress is stunning." She didn't add, revealing.

Isabella grinned and hugged Cate. "You think so? You are just the nicest ever. Come on, I think we'd better get going." She bustled them out of the bathroom and then seemed to forget Cate altogether at the sight of James.

Cate wondered at the power of love to so distract her friend. John was waiting with a small book in his hand. He eyed her up and down and then held out the stationary as if to tempt her.

"What is that?" she asked.

"I managed to sneak out a couple of dance cards," he said, coyly. "I took the liberty of filling in most of yours."

Cate couldn't stop a grimace, but she lowered her head, in the hopes he wouldn't notice.

"Th-thank you," she said. "But I don't think that's allowed."

John ran an arm along her neck and then grasped her proprietorially around her shoulder. "Such a good girl," he cooed.

Cate was grateful for the narrow hallway which forced them to walk single file. She wished she could wipe off her shoulder, but she refrained.

They rode the large elevator to the appropriate floor which opened to a grand hallway.

"This is my favourite part of the hotel," Isabella trilled. "It's so *expensive* looking." She was holding James' hand. He held her small red clutch for her.

The hallway opened into a tall-ceilinged room with a lounge off to one side. A half dozen hotel employees were set up at a long table. A line had already formed and they waited to hand in their tickets. When they made it to the table, a woman with two tight buns at either side of her head explained the rules.

"Here are your dance cards," she explained to the women as she passed out identical booklets to the one John had produced. They were small and cream-coloured with gold writing. There was a gold band which Cate saw Isabella place around her wrist.

"According to Regency custom, you should only dance two dances with one man," the woman continued. "Your partner at any given time is responsible for tending to you, so if you want punch or a plate of goodies, just ask. All of the dances are from the Regency era. There is always one couple to teach the dance in each grouping, so if you don't know the steps, just follow along."

She pointed them toward the next room, which was a long gallery with marble columns and an impressive stone fireplace. Huge window lined one wall, overlooking the mountains. There were tables of goodies scattered around the room and groups of people gathered to admire the offerings or just to visit.

Cate and Isabella stopped to gaze at an ice sculpture of a dancing couple. She noticed her brother and John picking up flutes of champagne at a table further on. Mrs. Thorpe had found some acquaintances who sampled chocolate-covered strawberries. Cate scanned the room hoping for a glimpse of the Tilneys, but could not spot them.

"You'd better be careful, Cate, or I'll tell my brother on you," Isabella teased.

Cate prickled at the suggestion of belonging to John. "It's such an elegant room," Cate said, instead.

They strolled along the rest of the hall to a smaller area with a huge chandelier and a grand piano where a man in a tuxedo played Christmas songs. She and Isabella found an empty window seat and were soon joined by John and James who offered them glasses of golden bubbles.

"Thank you," Cate nodded.

"I can't believe Tilney had to sing for his father tonight," John said too loudly. "His dad must be some kind of dictator. You wouldn't catch me acting like such a servant. I bet he doesn't even get paid."

Isabella laughed. "Can you imagine mom making us work for her?"

"I thought it was beautiful," Cate interjected.

"I suppose you're the same," John chucked her under the chin. "Doing whatever mommy tells you, am I right, James?"

Cate waited for her brother to stick up for her, but he was gazing into Isabella's eyes, smiling.

"I don't think helping a parent is anything to make fun of." Cate stood up, wiping imaginary crumbs off her dress.

John rose to take her elbow. "Well, now I've gone and made you mad," he said playfully. "I can't say I'm sorry. You look even sexier with those hot red cheeks. Why don't you give me that silly little dance book so I can toss it out."

"No thank you," Cate said and hurried toward the ladies room. She looked back, expecting Isabella to follow her, but she and James were wrapped up in some kind of fascinating topic while he played a lock of her hair around his finger.

Cate was so focussed on escaping from John that she didn't even look into the faces around her. "Cate!" she heard just as she reached the rest room.

She sniffed and turned to face Ellie Tilney.

"Oh!" she said, taken aback. "Hello. How are you?"

"Just fine," smiled Ellie. "But you don't look so good. Mind if I join you?"

Cate shook her head and the young woman followed her into the spacious room. Dainty couches ringed the outside of the room while a mirrored vanity took up one whole wall. Ellie motioned to a seat by the tall window and Cate sank down.

"You look lovely," Ellie said, sitting down in the couch opposite.

"So do you," Cate tried to smile.

"Do you mind if I ask what's bothering you?" Ellie asked, digging through her clutch until she pulled out a tissue.

Cate was horrified at the thought of repeating what John had said. "I guess it's the first time I've been away from my family for Christmas." She dabbed her nose.

"I'm so sorry," Ellie said. "You have your brother with you, though?"

"Yes. Yes. I'm just being silly. You see, my dad passed away a few years ago and my mom is all alone with my little brothers."

"Oh yes. I understand. We lost my mom when I was thirteen. You worry about your lonely parent."

"Yes," Cate nodded, feeling Ellie comprehended what she felt better than Isabella ever could. "Did your Dad never remarry?"

A dark look flitted through Ellie's eyes. "He's very busy," she said. "Very wrapped up in the hotel," she motioned as if to take in the entire building with her arm. "Even Henry and I find it quite consuming." She paused, thinking and then smiled warmly. "I hope you'll enjoy tonight, though. It's my pet project. Our one night to forget about all of our responsibilities and worries and pretend we're someone else. Someone more carefree."

Cate shook herself. "Of course! It's a wonderful idea." She rose and smoothed out her dress.

Ellie stood as well and bit her lip. "I hope you don't mind my interfering, but I think my brother would like to dance with you."

Cate felt her cheeks colour. "Oh, yes. That would be nice." She flinched at her own words. She felt it would be a lot more than nice, but didn't want to make this fine young woman uncomfortable, or her brother for that matter.

Ellie laughed softly. "I'll let him know. Would you mind coming with me to see him?"

Cate felt a little thrill through her limbs. "Yes, thank you."

The crowd parted to let the women pass through. Cate noticed how people nodded at Ellie and even bowed or curtseyed. They obviously knew who she was and were embracing the regency theme.

"Here they are," Ellie pointed to her brother and an older man. Cate recognized him from the Christmas carolling and could see the resemblance between him and Henry. They were both tall and dark-haired, though his father had some salt sprinkled among the pepper. However, where Henry looked relaxed and had a hint of mischief in his eyes, his father looked rigid and imposing.

"This is my father," Ellie tucked her hand into his elbow. "Reginald Tilney."

"How do you do," he said and held out his large hand for Cate to shake.

"Good, thank you," Cate noticed his eye twitch at her improper English. "I mean, well. I'm very well, thank you." She felt her neck heat up.

Henry stepped forward to take her elbow. "I hope you haven't completely filled your dance card yet," his eyes twinkled in the light of the chandeliers overhead.

"Not yet," she grinned, though the thought of John's fake dance card nagged her. "When does the dancing start?"

"Fairly soon, I think." Henry said. "What do you think, sis? Should we get this party started?"

Ellie laughed. It was easy to see she adored her brother. "If you say so. I'll go welcome the guests."

Ellie led the way on her father's arm and Cate and Henry followed behind. Once again, the crowd seemed to part for them and began to line up once they made it to the entrance of the ballroom.

Ellie leaned in to speak to someone dressed like a kind of guard waiting by the entrance. Then the man called out "General Tilney, Miss Tilney, Mr. Tilney and Miss Morland."

Cate jumped at his echoing voice and looked around her in surprise. How did he know her name? Then she noticed how the other guests spoke to him before he announced who they were.

She saw Ellie looking at her. "It's a regency tradition," she explained as they moved toward the centre of the room. "It was polite to announce your guests and to let everyone else know who was there. I hope you don't mind."

"No, no," Cate said. "I was just surprised."

"You'll find my sister is a bit of a nerd," Henry whispered loudly. "I apologize."

Ellie swatted her brother's arm. "If I'm a nerd about this, I shouldn't tell her about your obsession with books," she teased.

"Oh no!" Henry held his hands to his face in mock horror. "Don't tell the poor girl that I love reading."

"What kind of books?" Cate asked eagerly.

"What? You mean aren't completely disgusted?" Henry smiled. "Could this mean you actually enjoy literature?"

"Of course I do!" Cate said. "Why wouldn't I?"

"I'm so glad you feel that way," Henry took her hand and tucked it into the crook of his arm. "You wouldn't believe how many girls I meet who only read online. So, who are your favourite authors?"

The room began to fill with guests, each one announced by the man at the door. Cate felt somewhat embarrassed. Would he find her books childish and girly?"

"Well, there's The Hunger Games," she began.

"Of course!" Henry said. "What a great place to start. Incredible writing, engrossing plot. What else?"

"I really enjoyed the Lemony Snicket Series of Unfortunate Events," she continued haltingly. "But I was younger when I read those."

"Brilliant! Such an ingenious writer. Did you make it through the whole series?"

"I did. I couldn't stop. I kept waiting for the mystery to be solved."

"But as soon as one mystery was solved, ten more cropped up," Henry finished her thought.

"Exactly! And there was The Giver series."

"By Lois Lowry. Yes. I started reading it at school and I couldn't wait for the next book."

"It took so long for them to come out." Cate nodded vigorously. She paused then, wondering if she could trust him with her favourite. "I don't suppose you've heard of Diane Setterfield."

"What?" Henry nearly shouted. "You've even read The Thirteenth Tale? I didn't think anyone in Canada had ever heard of it."

"What do you mean?" Cate felt a little breathless.

"Just that I discovered it while I travelled in England two years ago. Almost everyone I met had read it there, but when I came back home, no one had heard of it. How did you find it?"

Before Cate could divulge her great love and respect for the book, John appeared at her side, holding out her fake dance card.

"Miss Morland, I believe you owe me this dance."

Cate had hardly noticed the music had started and couples were taking their places on the wooden floor.

"Oh. I. . ." Disappointment rushed through her body, leaving her feeling a bit limp.

Henry peered at the dance card with a look of surprise. "Miss Morland," he bowed to her and let John lead her away.

"I'll bet that spoiled good-for-nothing isn't used to being stood up like that," John sounded triumphant.

"I don't know why you had to interrupt us," Cate said with gritted teeth.

"Oh, I'm so sorry," John said with a huff. "I thought I was saving you from a boring conversation. I heard him talking about England as I approached and thought I was giving you an out." He dropped her hand as they made it to an opening in the dance formation.

"Excuuuuse me."

"It wasn't a boring conversation," she said, although her voice was quiet and John was distracted by the people around them. "It could have been one of the most interesting I've had in my life."

The music drowned out Cate's last statement so that even she couldn't hear it. Fortunately, a dance instructor was calling out the steps, because Cate had never even seen it before. She was instantly thankful for the years of social dance she'd taken in gym class. The jive and waltz were a far cry from these dances, but the counting of eight and relation to one's partner were familiar. Although she had felt angry with John a moment before, something about the movement and the group effort soon had her laughing at her own mistakes. Even though John was her partner, they rarely touched and she was traded between men like a baseball card, it seemed.

The first song ended and she clapped her hands, a bit breathless. John's mood; however, had worsened.

"I forgot how stupid this was," he sneered. Cate had noticed that his lack of musicality severely affected his ability to dance. Apparently his timing was as off as his pitch. "You may as well go find your queer little friend again. He can take care of the dancing, I'm sure."

Cate felt slightly offended that she was being so unceremoniously dumped and she really did wish to dance some more, but she said nothing and walked toward a corner away from the dancers. She tried to find Henry again, without appearing to be searching for him. He found her.

"Done so soon, Miss Morland?" he laughed. "Regency dancing not for you?" he said it with a rather good English accent.

"Actually, I liked it. My partner, no so much," her eyes crinkled in a smile.

"Excellent!" he made a mock bow toward her. "Then, may I have the pleasure of this dance."

"Certainly," Cate curtseyed in return and accepted his proffered hand.

Henry's musicality translated perfectly into excellent dancing. He was even able to talk whenever the dance allowed them to draw close together.

"I've had several young men ask me about you," he said, continuing with his English accent.

"Oh really?" Cate could hardly respond while she concentrated on the steps.

"Yes, I told them you hated men and couldn't possibly dance with them," he teased.

"What?" Cate lost her place and found herself on the wrong side of the dance.

"Just kidding. I told them your dance card was full, but that I'd put in a good word for them."

Cate struggled to get back into place and rhythm. "That wasn't my dance card," she managed to say.

"I know," Henry replied as they sashayed through a line of dancers. "My sister designed the booklets and made me approve the final product.

But I didn't want to rat you out."

The dance ended and the instructor called out directions for the next piece of music. "It wasn't my idea," Cate managed to say.

"I'm glad to hear that," Henry said. "I'd hate to think you were trying to ignore all of Ellie's hard work."

"No, I would never. . ." but Cate was cut off by the intricate dance pattern. Each dance seemed to get progressively more difficult. Or was it just that Henry distracted her concentration so greatly?

This dance was certainly quicker and Cate traded partners several times before finding Henry again. When they song ended, he bowed toward her and then offered his hand.

"It was a scandal in Regency time to dance more than two dances with the same person," he said, leading her toward a refreshment table.

"Really?" Cate was finding it difficult to breath. "How did anyone ever get to know anyone?" she said.

"You'd have to ask Ellie. It sounds like an extremely complicated process to me. Looks and money had more to do with it, I think."

"Not all that unlike today," Cate accepted the glass of champagne Henry passed her. Her head was already a bit buzzed from her first flute, but she was thirsty and grateful for something to do with her nervous hands.

Suddenly Isabella was at Cate's side, tapping her shoulder impatiently.

"Cate, I hope you're not going to ignore us all night," she said with a glorious smile that contradicted the ice in her words.

"Not at all. I was just. . ."

"John thought you were going to dance with him again," she said pointedly. "You don't mind, do you?" she batted her eyes at Henry.

"Of course," Henry said with a jaunty bow, but Cate thought she heard a hint of irritation in his voice.

Cate allowed herself to be pulled away by her friend, feeling guilty both for leaving Henry and for upsetting Isabella.

CHAPTER ELEVEN

John apparently had no intention of dancing any more that night. "What a stupid tradition this is," he sneered at the dancers from his perch at a table along the sidelines. "I suppose you like it, being a girl and everything."

Cate didn't feel up to making a response.

"At least I haven't wasted the whole evening," he continued, drinking steadily from a pint. "I met your little boyfriend's father."

"He's not my boyfriend," she blurted, but instantly wished she could take it back. He chuckled and continued. "General Reginald Tilney served in the British army. He retired before moving to Canada. It's too bad he didn't pass on some of his bravery to his wimpy son."

"He's not a wimp," Cate stuck in.

John rolled his eyes. "Any man who can't stand up to his own father. . . Anyway, I put in a good word for you, so you owe me there. I put in a good word for all of us. I think I impressed him, volunteering for the military. Your brother too. I bet he wishes his own son had such backbone."

Cate seethed at his words, but felt bound to sit with John for at least another ten minutes.

"He wants to meet you, so don't be surprised if he gets his son to introduce you two."

Cate wondered momentarily what John had told him, but had no time to ask before the General showed up at their table with Ellie and Henry in tow. John and Cate rose to greet him.

"General Tilney," John saluted him.

"At ease, Officer," the General replied. "Is this the young woman you told me about?" he smiled at her and held out his hand.

Cate shook it, nervously. "Catherine Morland, sir. Pleased to meet you."

"Call me Reginald. Are you enjoying yourself?"

"Very much . . . Reginald. Ellie has done an incredible job."

Ellie gave a strained smile at her father's side. "Thank you," she said. "I'm so glad you're enjoying yourself."

"I'm glad you've met my children," he continued. "They speak highly of you."

Cate was overwhelmed by the General's approval. She could only nod and smile.

"I hope you can join us for dinner December 26th," the General continued. "At our home."

Cate noticed Henry and Ellie were watching her as if they were holding their breath. She smiled brightly. "I'd love to. Thank you. I'll just have to make sure it is alright with . . ."

"Mr. and Mrs. Allen. By all means. You may confirm at this number." General Tilney produced a platinum case from his breast pocket and handed Cate a business card. "My personal number," he added.

Cate was flustered. "Thank you. That's very kind."

"I could pick you up from your room," Henry said.

"Or, perhaps if you're free, you could join us for some skiing tomorrow," Ellie said.

John interjected. "No, I'm sorry, but we've already booked Cate for skiing," he said. "We've been begging her to come for days," he added. "We've got her now, and I'm afraid we can't let her out of it."

"We wouldn't ask that of her," Henry said.

"But I never said I'd go skiing with you tomorrow," Cate was finally able to interject.

John threw up his hands, as if exasperated. "There she goes again!" he boomed. "I tell you," he said conspiratorially to the General. "I'm starting to think she's afraid of the slopes. I don't think she's ever been skiing."

Ellie put a hand on her shoulder. "They can be intimidating. We usually stick to cross-country, ourselves. We'll see if we can ask you another time."

Cate wanted to say more. She knew she had never agreed to go skiing with John, but they all believed she had. She could see General Tilney was prepared to move on, taking his children with him. She would try to speak to Ellie or Henry about it again later.

"Well, aren't you the popular one," John said after a long pull from his beer. "Trying to get out of skiing," he shook his head.

"But you never asked me for tomorrow," she exclaimed.

"Sure I did. You're just so terrified of looking like an idiot that you've blocked it from your memory."

Cate stood up to make her point more clear. "I have not. You lied to them and you're trying to lie to me. I'm going to tell Henry that I can go cross-country skiing."

John stood up and grasped her arm. "Calm down, little lady," he whispered. "So maybe I hadn't asked you, but Isabella and James have already planned to go and they want you and me to go with them. You can't let your brother down."

"But I don't want to go skiing with you, and more importantly, I can't lie to my new friends," she shook off his hand.

John slumped into his seat, looking dejected. "I see we're not good enough for you anymore, now that you've met your new, rich friends." He finished his beer in a gulp. "And after all I've done for you, talking you up to that General. If it weren't for me, I bet you wouldn't even be invited to ski with them tomorrow."

Cate sat down, heavily. "What did you say to him about me?"

John sneered. "Ah, so now you're interested in me again. I told him how great you were. He wanted to know about your situation."

"What situation?"

Before John could answer, Isabella and James arrived at the table, breathless and laughing.

"That dancing is hilarious!" Isabella's shrill voice interrupted all other attempts at conversation. "I don't think James and I got a single step right!"

"Isabella's just being nice," James countered. "I'm sure she could have done it if it weren't for me."

Isabella waved at a waiter who refreshed their drinks. "Maybe if it weren't for all the alcohol." She seemed to notice Cate for the first time. "Well, don't you look like a woman scorned. What have you done to her, John?" she poked her brother playfully.

John held up his hands as if to say he was completely innocent. "All I did was tell her about our plans to ski tomorrow. You'd think I told her she was due for the firing squad."

James slid an arm around her shoulders. "Don't worry, sis. We'll take good care of you."

"But you never asked me before and John told the Tilneys you had and that I'd already agreed."

"Oh the Tilneys," Isabella said with a wave of disgust. "I'm sick to death of hearing about the Tilneys. They can't have you all the time and whether we asked you yet or not, we need you to come skiing with us tomorrow. Besides, it's Christmas." Isabella smiled so sweetly that Cate wavered a moment.

She stood up. "I have to tell them the truth," she said and moved away before anyone could convince her otherwise.

It took several minutes for her to locate Henry. She found him dancing with Isabella and stopped to watch them. They both performed the complicated dance perfectly. Of course, they'd probably been practicing for years, but it was delightful to watch. She clapped when they finished and they both came directly over to her.

"That was incredible," she grinned.

"Oh, it's really nothing," Ellie waved away her compliment. "We've just had some practice and once you've done it a few times, it gets much easier."

"I had to tell you that John was not exactly telling the truth. My friends never asked me to go skiing. I think they intended to, but they never actually did ask. I can go cross-country skiing with you tomorrow. I'd like to very much." She said it so quickly, she wondered if they even understood her.

Henry and Ellie exchanged glances. "It's really okay," Ellie said. "We realize Christmas is a special day. We can do it some other day. It's no problem."

"I just didn't want you to think I'd lie to you," she said. "I hate lies. I don't really think John intended to lie. He must have thought he already asked."

"You think that because you think everyone is like you," Henry said gently. "You would never tell a lie on purpose and so you can't imagine anyone else doing the same. You're like a breath of fresh air."

Cate felt herself blush. "Oh, I'm sure I'm not all that. I . . . I . . ."

"Could I have the pleasure of one more dance," Henry bowed to her.

"Yes, thank you," Cate said.

The next dance was simpler and she was able to stay beside Henry the whole time. She noticed Isabella dancing with a tall, handsome man in uniform.

"Who's that?" she blurted, before she realized how rude she must sound.

"Ah, that is my brother. He's finally made it."

"Why is he dancing with Isabella?" she asked.

Henry chuckled. "Well, she does have a certain kind of attraction for some men, I suppose. Just the sort my brother would go for, actually."

"Oh," Cate was perplexed. "I hope she'll tell him she's with my brother. I would hate for his heart to be broken."

"If your brother and Isabella are together, I'm sure there's nothing to worry about," Henry smiled, but his eyes looked grim. "My brother isn't looking for a relationship."

Cate squinted at him, trying to discern what he was saying. It was just a dance. She tried to shake off her concern and enjoy her time with Henry.

CHAPTER TWELVE

Although her muscles ached in strange places and she felt exhausted, Cate could not cross over into sleep. Just when she was about to fall, the image of General Tilney or John Thorpe would come to mind. What had he told him? John's sneering laugh as he lied to the entire Tilney family about Cate's plans would float through her eyelids, taunting her and bringing her out in a cold sweat. And when she thought she had finally banished those thoughts, a niggling worry about Henry's brother dancing with Isabella would gnaw at her mind. For tonight at least, all thoughts of ghosts were vanquished, unless you considered these ghosts of memory. Or ghosts of things to come?

Christmas morning had always been an early, bustling affair at the Morland household, but at the Banff Springs hotel, the muted silence of thick carpets and long drapes continued well past 10 a.m. Cate was showered and pacing when Robin tapped on her door at last.

"Merry Christmas!" she said brightly, when Cate let her in. Robin was holding several shiny packages stacked on top of one another. "Where should we open these?"

Cate joined her friend in surveying their lush hotel room. They both gazed at the fireplace. "Over there," Cate pointed.

Robin and Gerald were dressed in Christmas bathrobes and had a tray of coffee on a table. Cate poured herself a cup and helped herself to a scone. Then they pulled arm chairs together around the fire.

"I hope your mother doesn't mind too much that we have you," Robin smiled apologetically.

"I'll phone her soon. She probably couldn't even hear it above the racket the boys are making right now anyway." She sipped her steaming cup, grateful for the warmth and caffeine.

"Why don't you begin?" Gerald held out a small green package.

"Your mom sent this with us."

Cate noticed her stocking had also been hung and filled by the fireplace. She opened the paper carefully and sighed when she saw the little necklace and matching earrings blinking up at her.

"Thanks Mom," she whispered. "Your turn, Robin."

They continued opening the rather embarrassingly large collection of presents for the next hour. She had never spent so long unwrapping gifts in her life.

"Thank you for all this," she said at last and handed her friends a thin envelop. "It isn't much, but I thought you'd like it."

"Oh, you didn't need to get us anything," Robin grew serious. "Your company is our gift." But she opened the thin envelope and pulled out two tickets to a concert at the Banff Springs.

"It's tomorrow night," Cate said. "A string quartet. I thought you'd enjoy it."

Robin hugged her and then Gerald. "Such a thoughtful girl," he said, patting her back. "Thank you."

The Allens excused themselves to have showers and Cate reached for the phone when it rang at her. "Hello?" she said.

"Time to go, sis," her brother greeted her.

"But it's Christmas morning," she said.

"Exactly. It's the perfect Christmas activity. Dress warm. We'll rent you some skis at the hill, unless you'd rather snowboard."

"No!" she almost shouted.

"I'm just teasing," he chuckled. "Be ready in 5." He hung up before she could tell him she needed to call home. But she got ready anyway. She couldn't disappoint her brother.

John had rented a car for their excursion. Isabella and James snuggled up in the back while Cate was left to sit up front with John. "I hate taking those ski buses," he sniffed.

"Are you having a good Christmas?" Cate asked, both to be polite and to divert the conversation from John's snobbery.

"Just another day," John waved his hand in the air. "We should have gotten an earlier start, I hope the hill isn't too busy. I wanted to leave at 7, but Isabella insisted we have a fancy breakfast and open our presents," he sneered. "Women!"

Cate took a deep breath. She looked back at her brother to remind herself why she'd come along. He was looking deeply into Isabella's eyes. They seemed to be discussing something personal, so she looked away again. She did not feel satisfied that she was doing what was best for him. Why had Isabella danced so closely to Henry's brother?

"You don't have anything to worry about, Cate," John was still talking.

"I've had plenty of practice teaching girls to ski. I guarantee you'll enjoy yourself," he winked at her.

Cate squirmed. "I think I'll sign up for a lesson first," she said.

John hit the steering wheel causing the car to swerve slightly as it cruised too fast through downtown Banff. "Don't be ridiculous, Cate. I've got it all planned out. Those pansy ski instructors don't challenge you at all. No, you'll learn from me!"

Cate rubbed her temples. Christmas was quickly turning on her. "No, I won't," she said through gritted teeth. "I'm taking lessons."

"Morland!" John shouted. "Talk some sense into your sister. She thinks some yahoo at the ski hill can teach her to ski better than I can."

James squeezed her shoulder. "He's really good, Cate. He taught me."

"And me," Isabella piped in. "He's the best."

"I'll only do it if you two promise to stay with us," Cate countered. She was not going to spend the day alone with John while her brother and Isabella made out somewhere on the hill.

"Of course we will!" Isabella said smoothly. "We're a team!"

Isabella's promise lasted for all of fifteen minutes.

"You're doing splendidly!" she trilled. "I'm just going to try out the Strawberry Chair with James and we'll meet you at the bottom."

Cate was still struggling to make it up and down the "Mighty Mite" section with John shouting instructions at her.

"No!" she shouted.

James patted her shoulder. "It's just one run, sis. It won't take long and then I bet you'll be ready to join us."

"I guarantee it!" John said confidently, with a commanding arm around her shoulders.

Cate let John keep his arm around her shoulders only so that she wouldn't fall down . . . again.

After John was distracted by several young women asking for pointers, Cate excused herself to go to the lodge. She had trouble getting her skis off, but eventually she peeked at another woman removing her skis and found out the secret to popping them out of her boots. Then she lugged her awkward boots up the dozens of steel stairs and heaved herself into the warm lodge. She bought a hot chocolate a found a seat by the window where she sat down, relieved. Then she looked at her watch and was dismayed to find they had only spent forty-five minutes at the hill, so far.

Cate enjoyed watching the skiers out the window. She chastised herself for not being able to catch on to the sport. It looked so easy. Maybe if she had a better teacher.

An hour or so later, she was mustering up the courage to head back out. Maybe she could pay for a lesson. Then she noticed her brother coming in the door with Isabella.

"James!" she stood up and waved her hands. Isabella squealed and practically skipped over to her table. Cate wondered how she was able to look so light and graceful in those clunky ski boots.

Isabella hugged her when she got there and then held out her left hand which sported a small glinting diamond.

"We're engaged!" she squealed again. "It was so romantic. He waited until I'd fallen on one of the slopes, then skied right up to me and got down on one knee. Oh Cate!" she hugged her again. "We're going to be sisters!"

Cate looked at her brother quizzically over Isabella's shoulder. He was beaming.

"Congratulations," she said it too slowly. "Wow, this is a surprise. I had no idea."

James clasped her hand and kissed her cheek. "I still can't believe she said yes."

"Does Mom know?" she asked.

"Not yet," James took out his cell phone. "Do you think I should call her now?"

Cate had no idea what her mom would say or think. How could James afford to get married when he was paying for his University degree by joining the army? It would be years before he had a well-paying job and he was still so young.

"If you think so," she said. She was glad she wasn't the one making the call.

James must have had a similar thought. He put his cell phone back in his pocket. "There probably isn't very good coverage here. I'll call her tonight."

Isabella chattered on while James bought them soup and sandwiches from the canteen. While he was gone, she whispered, "I would never have said yes if it weren't for the Allens. Weddings are so expensive."

"The Allens?" Cate said, surprised, but before she could ask more, John showed up.

"There you are," he said grandly. "Trying to hide away, are you? You've got to keep at it, Cate. You don't get better by sitting in the lodge."

"Oh leave her alone," Isabella patted her brother. "I just got engaged!" she showed off her ring, leaving Cate to wonder how her brother had paid for it.

"The dirty scamp," John exclaimed. "So he did find the courage. Next thing you know, Cate will be expecting a ring," he winked at her.

"I will not!" she retorted, but her brother returned with lunch and there was a lot of back slapping and mockery to be had.

After lunch, Isabella insisted she take Cate under her wing. "I'm so sorry I left you alone, but I had an inkling that James had something to say to me. I never dreamed it was this, well I did hope, but I thought I'd give him a chance to say it away from prying eyes. He's such a shy boy, when you get to know him. At first, I thought he was just a tough soldier, but underneath, he's a real softy."

Cate could relax with Isabella at least and was able to make it down the beginner slope a few times with only one or two falls. Isabella was a patient teacher as long as she could talk. Cate wanted to interject and ask what Isabella meant about the Allens, but the skiing took most of her concentration and Isabella barely paused for breath, so she left the question unasked.

By late afternoon, she was ready to join the men on the Angel slope. The chair lift was high and fast and she felt her nerves and fear returning. She couldn't speak, only nodding and murmuring if she had to answer a question. They all fit on the ski lift. She was sandwiched between Isabella and John.

She read a sign just before the top of the hill "Ski Tips Up!" and lifted hers as high as they would go.

"Not that high," Isabella patted her knee. "Just watch me." She followed her lead and John helped to guide her off the lift. They turned her the right direction and she made it to the top of the hill.

"Try to breathe more slowly," Isabella looked concerned. "I'll stay right beside you. John, are you sure we're not rushing her?"

"Too late now," he said, reassuringly. "Last one down's a rotten egg!" he pointed his skis down and took off.

"Show off," muttered Isabella. "James, you stay right with us. We need to take care of your sister."

Cate relaxed somewhat with John out of view and her brother and Isabella's encouragement. Somehow, she survived and made it down the mountain.

CHAPTER THIRTEEN

Cate groaned when she woke the next morning.

"How am I going to cross-country ski today?" she asked the high-vaulted ceiling.

A warm shower helped and when Robin suggested a massage first thing in the morning, she jumped at the idea.

"Your brother certainly is smitten with Isabella," Robin said with her eyes closed on the massage table. They were having their treatments in the same room.

"He's very devoted to her," Cate said into her massage table.

"You sound like you have something on your mind," Robin replied.

Cate paused a moment to consider how best to say what she was feeling. "It's just that I don't know if she loves him as much as he loves her. She always says how much she loves him, but the way she danced with Henry's brother the other night. . .I don't know."

Robin's masseuse instructed her to turn onto her back, making her much easier to understand. "Not every girl is as loyal as you are," she waved her hands in the air and the massage therapist had to leap out of the way to avoid being smacked. "Sorry!" Robin said. "Some women enjoy a little flirtation now and then. I doesn't mean anything."

"I guess," Cate murmured.

Henry insisted that Cate not pay for her ski rentals. "You're our guest," he said. "We get free rentals anyway and today you're one of the family."

She felt warmed by the statement. Once they had their equipment, Ellie, Henry and she walked down a mountain of stairs and across a bridge to the snow-covered golf-course.

"We could have started at the other end," Ellie explained. "It's not nearly as far a walk, but then you would just have to walk up all those stairs on the way back."

"It's a gorgeous day," Cate said, trying to ignore her quivering muscles. She had a sneaking suspicion she would be just as bad at cross country skiing as she was at downhill.

"These are waxless skis, so we can just snap them on and get going right away," Henry explained.

Cate had no idea what he was talking about.

Henry and Isabelle were kind and patient teachers. They let her practice on the flat golf course until she figured out the rhythm.

"I think I've got it!" Cate surprised herself.

"You're a natural," Henry grinned as if he were proud of her.

"I'm afraid the first part is a bit tricky," Isabelle sounded worried. "Henry, are you sure we should do the entire trail? It's her first time."

"We'll take it slow," he said. "We can always turn back if we need to."

They crossed the golf course into the forest. Tracks had been set in the thick snow and they veered left directly toward a steep hill.

"Ummm," Cate furrowed her brow, taking in the long assent. "I don't know..."

"Don't worry about it. Ellie will go first so you can watch how she does it and I'll go behind in case you need any help."

The thought of Henry watching her ski was no comfort, but she followed Ellie and surprised herself with her ability. After several minutes of diligent effort, they reached the top of the first hill and Ellie turned to smile at her.

"If you can do that, the rest of the ski will seem like a breeze!"

"This snow is perfect," Henry announced. "Not too sticky and not too icy."

They continued on and Cate was able to look up from the ground long enough to take in their incredible surroundings. The path followed the shape of the river. They were already quite high above the water. Beyond the river rose a tall craggy mountain layered in coniferous trees and snow.

To the left was more forest and another mountain. Cate felt they had left civilization, but when they stopped for a sip of water, she could still make out the elegant hotel behind them.

"How are you feeling?" Ellie said with concern. "Do you think you can keep going?"

Cate was surprised to discover her aching muscles no longer bothered her. She felt a slight discomfort in her feet, but no longer dreaded skiing. "This is a good pace for me," she said. "Downhill was way too fast."

Ellie exchanged glances with her brother. "There is some downhill up ahead," she cautioned. "Not like at the ski hills, but it can get a bit fast. You can watch me when we get there and let me know if it's okay."

There were two sets of tracks along the path. One for coming and one for going, but there were very few skiers coming toward them, so Ellie and Henry took turns skiing beside her.

"So, about our favourite author," Henry said as he skied beside her.

"Oh yes! I was hoping we could talk about The Thirteenth Tale again!" She was so excited that she lost her grip on her pole and it went flying up ahead of them.

"Don't worry, I'll get it back," Henry said in his best Superman impression.

Cate giggled. Once she had her pole back, she continued. "I've been reading it while we're here. I feel like I can really imagine the ancient house while I'm staying in the old hotel. I can feel what she feels and imagine the traces of ghosts."

"Is that right?" Henry lifted an eyebrow. "I don't suppose you've seen any of our famous spectres during your stay."

Cate felt slightly embarrassed. It was one thing to hear strange noises in the middle of the night in her darkened room. It was another to admit it in the bright sunshine and frosty white air of morning. "It was probably nothing."

"No, tell me!" Henry said. "I love hearing about them."

Cate stalled. "Have you ever seen anything?"

"You're not getting off that easy, young lady," he shook his head. "Tell me!"

"It was just noises," Cate attempted.

"What kind of noises?" he probed.

"Knocking on my door. At 3 in the morning."

"Anything else?" he looked eager.

"You're going to make fun of me, I know it."

"I won't!" he held up his index and middle finger together and crossed his heart. "I don't know if that's the right sign, but I want to know."

"I felt breathing on my face," she shivered at the memory. "And I heard a voice."

"Oh good!" he said. "What did it say?"

"Well, I really think I was just dreaming."

"Come on, tell me!" He looked like one of her little brothers begging to know what he was getting for his birthday.

She took a deep breath and replied, "Too late."

"Too late? You aren't going to tell me?"

"No, it said 'Too Late'."

"Too late," Henry mused. "For what, I wonder? Did that mean anything to you?"

"I don't know. It's stupid. I can't believe I'm telling you this. You're going to think I'm ridiculous."

Henry didn't say anything else for a while. Cate wondered what he was thinking, but was afraid he was just realizing what a waste of his time she was. Then he said;

"I really think I should take you to my mother's house."

Cate was more than surprised by this statement. "Your mother?"

"Yes, I believe Ellie told you she passed away nine years ago."

"Yes," Cate said.

"She had a house which belonged to her family which now belongs to us.

"What a lovely memory to have," Cate replied.

"I think she would have liked you," Henry said.

Cate felt honoured.

They skied in silence for some time and then met up with Ellie who had found a picnic table and was taking a thermos, mugs and cookies out of her pack.

Cate survived the downhill parts and greatly enjoyed the view of the river in the valley of the towering mountains. They made it around the entire loop and returned as the sky began to darken.

"Thank you," she said after they had returned their ski equipment. "It was perfect."

Henry squeezed her shoulder. "We'll meet you at your room at six," he said. "You did a great job of our old-fashioned sport."

Cate hardly remembered the walk up to her room. Her mind was too busy with little hopes and memories.

CHAPTER FOURTEEN

The Allens were enthusiastic about Cate's dinner with the Tilneys.

"I've always wondered what their house looks like from the inside," Robin sighed from her seat on the chaise by the hotel window. "You can see it from the spa. It's set back in the trees, probably the eastern most building allowed in the park. There are spires and windows everywhere. You'll have to tell me all about it."

"Reg Tilney keeps to himself," Gerald interjected. "I've never heard of him having guests to his house. You must have made quite an impression on the old man."

Cate blushed. She hoped it wasn't the old man she'd made such an impression on. She felt nervous.

"I hope I use the right cutlery and everything," she stammered.

Robin squeezed her shoulder. "Of course you will. You'll be perfect. I'll help you with your hair."

Cate hopped into the shower to freshen up and soothe her tired muscles.

Henry and Ellie knocked on their hotel room precisely on time.

"Come in!" Gerald was effusive. "Can I get you two something to drink?" He made a move toward the minibar.

Ellie's forehead crumpled in concern and she looked at her brother.

"Thank you, Mr. Allen," Henry nodded his head. "I'm afraid our father is quite a perfectionist," he chuckled, but his eyes were serious. "He doesn't like to wait for his supper."

"Well, who does?" Gerald said, good-naturedly. "Have you got everything, Catherine?"

Cate lifted up her small purse to prove she had and then hugged her hosts goodnight.

"I'll see you later. Enjoy the concert!" she smiled and waved.

Henry and Ellie walked quickly, guiding her through the labyrinth hallways of the hotel into the crisp night air.

"I hope you don't mind a little walk," Henry said. "I'm afraid we're going to completely exhaust you today."

"Not at all," Cate tried to disguise her breathlessness. "It's a beautiful night!"

They followed the streetlit sidewalk until its end and then continued down a long winding driveway hidden behind guard-like pine trees. Only small garden lights lit the way. Cate was grateful for a nearly full moon to help them.

"My father likes to keep this house a secret," Ellie said. "It was a Catholic Abbey at one point, before the hotel took it over."

"How interesting," Cate remarked, imagining a line of nuns walking the same path they took. After several minutes, she finally saw the house. Mansion was more like it. It was a massive, stone building with towers and a wide lawn. Unlike the hotel, there were no cheery Christmas lights to brighten the dark rock. She felt a shiver of dread come over her, but she shook it off.

"It's a hazard of the trade," Henry said. "You find that after a day of serving everyone, all you want is your privacy." He opened the tall wooden doors and gestured for Cate to enter.

She followed him in, trying to absorb the grandeur before her. She had never been in a home with such a large entryway. She was used to the tiny closet and shoe-strewn 'mudrooms' of her neighbours, not this high-ceilinged hall with fresh-cut flowers sitting on top of stylish pedestals. There wasn't a shoe or closet in sight. She wondered what they did with them.

"Don't worry about your shoes," Ellie instructed.

"But I'm wearing boots," she was embarrassed by her snowy footwear.

Ellie pointed out an ornate shoe rack tucked into the corner and then showed her a basket of slippers.

Henry looked at his watch as if he was agitated. "Dad will be expecting us," he said. "I'll have to give you the tour after supper, if that's okay?"

"Of course," Cate felt some of his nerves wash off on her. She would hate to make the General wait.

"Ah, there you are," he said in a clipped voice when they entered the dining room. "I was beginning to think you weren't coming."

"It's only just six," Ellie said gently. "You remember Cate Morland," she nodded.

"Welcome to our humble home," he came toward her and shook her hand. "I suppose you don't think it very large after being a regular guest of the Allens."

"Oh no!" she exclaimed. "This is – magnificent!"

"Well, we only live in a small town," General Tilney sounded apologetic. "We don't have the easy access to the big city, like they do."

"You have a beautiful home," Cate said as Henry pulled out a chair for her. She gazed at the plethora of dinnerware before her. A servant entered with a bottle of champagne. She allowed him to pour her a glass, but promised herself she wouldn't drink it all. She would hate to get silly in front of these sophisticated people.

"When the hotel opened, there was no such thing as oil money," the General began. "It was the railway that brought people to Banff. The hotel was much smaller then, but I think it has become a respectable establishment over the years."

Cate wondered why he seemed to put his hotel down in front of her. "We have greatly enjoyed our stay," she said. "The spa is fantastic."

The General harrumphed and accepted a bowlful of soup. Cate watched Ellie before choosing the correct spoon to enjoy her bowl. "Yum!" she couldn't help exclaiming over the spicy pumpkin bisque.

"We have an excellent cook," Ellie sounded on edge. Cate wondered at the change in her friends. They seemed less comfortable in their own home than they did anywhere else.

Cate was glad she'd worked up an appetite skiing. The meal kept on coming. There was a salad, beef tenderloin, risotto, mussels, and fruit sorbet. General Tilney excused himself and encouraged her to enjoy the company of his children. They visibly relaxed once their father left the room.

"Ready to see the rest of the place?" Ellie asked once they'd finished their tea.

"Absolutely!" she nearly clapped her hands at the prospect and the change in mood.

"The house is over 100 years old," Henry said as they passed out of the dining room into a large sitting room. The floors were rich, dark wood and the windows were tall and heavily draped. "Our father likes to keep the authenticity of the age," he continued. "The previous owner did a lot to modernize the house, but Dad did a complete renovation when we moved in to remove almost everything modern."

"Not the electricity, of course," Ellie chuckled. "Thank goodness!"

The rooms were expensively furnished, but struck Cate as dark and uncomfortable. There was a library, several other sitting rooms and a large hall with a grand piano. "You must have wonderful parties here," Cate remarked.

"Once in a while," Henry replied.

"Not since mother died," Ellie said quietly. "She loved parties.

Especially at Christmas."

Cate felt the weight of her words. "That must be why you're so good at organizing the Christmas Eve Ball," she said, hoping to cheer her friend.

She was satisfied by Ellie's small smile. "Thank you."

"The bedrooms are all upstairs," Henry said. "I'll let my sister show you around up there. I'll meet you back in the games room, if you'd like to play a little pool."

Cate felt a bit embarrassed. "If you'll teach me. I've never played for real. Just the games my brothers make up at the community hall sometimes."

"Well, maybe you could teach me then," Henry smiled and disappeared down the hallway.

"Do you want to see the bedrooms?" Ellie asked. "We don't have to."

"Oh yes!" Cate said. "I love old houses and I've never been in one this big before. I bet the rooms are beautiful."

They mounted a wide, winding staircase. "I'm afraid they're just plain old rooms," Ellie said.

There was a large window at the top of the staircase overlooking the forest, river and mountains. Cate sighed. "What a view!"

Ellie grinned. "Yes. I've always thought how lucky we are to live here. I'll show you my room first."

Ellie's accommodations included a sitting room with a fireplace attached by French doors to a large bedroom with a canopy bed, followed by a private bathroom with an antique clawfoot bathtub.

"This is amazing!" Cate said. She was drawn to a floor to ceiling shelf of books.

Ellie joined her at the shelf. "Some of them are a little embarrassing," she nodded at a collection of V.C. Andrews books. "I just can't get rid of them."

"Don't be embarrassed around me. There are some books you just can't put down."

"Have you finished The Thirteenth Tale?" she asked.

"Not yet! I keep trying to stay away to finish, but with all the skiing and dancing I've been doing lately, I can hardly keep my eyes open."

Ellie laughed. "Come, I'll show you the guest rooms and maybe my brothers' rooms, if they aren't too messy," she rolled her eyes.

While they returned to the hallway with its many pieces of artwork, Ellie asked. "How much longer are you staying in Banff?"

"Just tonight and tomorrow and then we'll head back," Cate paused to look at a small painting of a cottage in the woods.

"So soon!" Ellie said. "I guess I shouldn't be surprised. No one stays at the hotel for long."

She showed her into a room very similar to her own, but without the personal effects or the large library.

"I wonder. . ." Ellie began.

"What?" Cate asked, turning to look at her friend.

"Well, it's probably much too soon. You don't have to."

"Don't have to what?" Cate pressed.

"Well, I thought maybe you could stay here after the Allens leave. But I'm sure you miss your family and want to get back. . ."

"Oh!" Cate was surprised. "I don't know. . ."

Ellie waved her hand dismissively. "Forget I said anything. You really don't have to."

"No. That would be incredible. I'd love to."

"Won't your mother miss you?" Ellie asked, her eyes sparkling a little.

"I'm sure she wouldn't mind. I see her all year long. A little longer couldn't hurt. I'll have to ask to make sure, but what about your father?"

"Oh," Ellie looked flustered. "He won't mind. He sort of suggested it, actually, but I didn't think you'd want to."

Cate hugged her friend. "Why would you think that? Thank you for the invitation. It would be my honour to stay here."

They toured several more rooms, including Henry's. Cate was pleased to note that he had twice as many books as his sister. They avoided General Tilney's and a room right next to it.

"What room is this?" Cate asked.

"That was my mother's," Ellie said softly. "We keep it closed."

Cate felt a little stirring of curiousity. "Really? Does no one go in then?"

Ellie took her time answering. "Sometimes I go in, to remember her. But I think my father would rather we didn't. He wouldn't want me to take you there." She looked around her, as if checking that no one was watching them. Then she spoke in a whisper. "Maybe if you stay here, I would have the chance to take you."

Cate felt humbled by her friend's trust. She smiled at her. "I'm so sorry you lost your mother. That must have been very difficult."

"Yes," Ellie rubbed at her cheek. "But you would know. Didn't you lose your father?"

"A few years ago. It was like our world went blank for a while."

"Yes," Ellie agreed. "I was thirteen when she passed away. I was away on a trip with some friends. I didn't get to say goodbye."

Cate patted her friend's back. "That's awful. How sad."

"My mom was the light in this house. It grew very dark when she died. I don't know what I would do without Henry."

Cate nodded. "I feel the same way about James."

Ellie dabbed at her eyes with a tissue. "But let's talk about other things. It's Christmastime. Let's go play some pool."

The games room was tucked into the back corner of the main floor. The pool table didn't even take up half the space. There was still room for card tables and cases filled with high end chess boards, checker boards and other games Cate didn't recognize. Henry was hooking up his iPod to a stereo hidden behind a large wooden door.

"Dad didn't want anyone to see the electronics in our house," Ellie said when they entered. "All of our T.V.'s, music and gaming systems are disguised as something antique."

Jason Gray crooned softly from hidden speakers. Henry rubbed his hands together.

"The cues are all chalked and ready to go. Now teach us this new form of pool. I can't wait to learn."

Cate bit her lip nervously. "It's really not pool at all. I think you'd better teach me the real rules."

"Maybe another time," Henry grinned. "Right now, I'm dying to play something new."

Cate shrugged. "Well, we call it party pool," she said. "You don't even need pool cues."

Henry's lifted his eyebrows. "Go on."

Cate positioned herself in front of the pool table and grasped the white ball. "One person rolls the ball across the table," she motioned without actually doing it. "The next person has to run around the table one time before the white ball stops moving and then they can roll the ball across the table," she ended lamely. "It's better with more people. I have such a large family."

"Awesome," Henry said. "Let's give it a try."

"I'll close the door," Ellie apologized. "We don't want to disturb Dad."

Ellie and Henry were surprisingly competitive. Cate soon forgot her embarrassment over the game in her effort to keep the white ball moving. She was encouraged by Henry's laughter to go all out and found herself the winner at the end.

"That was fantastic!" Henry said, breathing heavily. "I've never been breathless after a game of billiards in my life. What did you think, Ellie?"

Ellie laughed. "That was a riot. We'll have to teach Frederick."

A grandfather clock chimed eleven o'clock somewhere nearby.

"Shoot! Is that the time already? We'd better get you back home before you turn into a pumpkin," Henry said.

"I don't think it was Cinderella that turned into the pumpkin," Cate replied.

"Right you are!" Henry chuckled. "Want a hot chocolate for the walk home?"

They made the hot drink in to-go mugs in a huge kitchen filled with stainless steel. Then they gathered their coats and boots and trudged out into the nearly moonless night.

CHAPTER FIFTEEN

Cate finally had the chance to speak with her mother for a few minutes the following day. "So, you're sure these are good people?" her mother asked.

"Yes. The Allens have met them. They own the hotel. General Tilney is a bit scary, but I'd mostly be hanging out with Ellie and Henry."

"How old is Henry?" her mother sounded wary.

"Twenty, I think. He's in art school, but mostly I'd be with Ellie. It's not like that Mom."

"Hmmm," her mother was quiet for a bit. Cate held her breath. "How will you get back? The Allens drove you to Banff, but you can't expect them to come back for you. Your brother won't be there either."

"I'm sure the Tilneys will take care of that."

"But you don't know for sure. I don't know if this is really the best idea. . ."

"Please Mom?" Cate did her best not to sound like one of her little brother's begging for a toy.

"You're almost done high school, honey. I guess you need to start making decisions for yourself. If the Allens approve of them, they must be okay."

"Oh, thank you!" Cate gushed. "Thanks Mom. I'm sorry I'm not there to help out. I promise you can put me right to work when I get back."

"Just make sure you're back a few days before school starts," her mom cautioned. "You don't want to be too worn out when you start up again."

"I will be. I mean, I won't. Yes mom. I'll be back before school starts, absolutely."

Cate was surprised her mom didn't bring up her brother's engagement, and she didn't want to be the one to introduce the subject. Perhaps her brother hadn't told her yet. It seemed strange, but she didn't want to lose her chance to stay with the Tilneys.

Robin and Gerald took her up the Sulphur Mountain Gondola where they had lunch in a large restaurant full of windows.

"It's nothing fancy, as far as food goes," Gerald stated. "But the view is hard to beat."

The town of Banff was miniscule beneath them. Even the Banff Springs Hotel looked like a little toy castle. After they had lunch and took a little walk around the trails, they rode the gondola down the mountain and stopped to have a soak in the Upper Hot Springs.

"This is my kind of spa," Gerald sighed while he closed his eyes and leaned into the steaming waters.

Robin did not look as relaxed. "There are so many people," she said with a hint of disdain when a child swam by and splashed her. "I don't know why you don't like the hotel spa. It's so much more dignified."

Gerald chuckled at his wife and kissed her cheek good-naturedly. "My little flower," he teased.

When they returned to the hotel, there was a message waiting for Cate. "Please come see me immediately!" It was Isabella. Cate hurried to hang up her swimsuit and tried to brush through her tangled hair before she rushed to Isabella's room.

"What is it?" she said breathlessly. Their room was in a state of upheaval. There were clothes strewn about the hotel room and Isabella's mother seemed to be trying to arrange things for packing.

"Let's go for tea," Isabella rolled her eyes at her nearly-panicked mother.

They walked together to The Rundle Lounge where Isabella ordered a pomegranate cocktail and a fruit plate, while Cate stuck with a pot of tea. The prices were exorbitant.

"What is it?" Cate asked once the waitress disappeared.

"Well, of course I'm not worried about myself in the least, but your brother drove home this morning to tell your mother about our engagement. He thought it would be best to speak to her himself before he introduced me."

Cate nodded. She must have called before her brother made it home.

"She gave us her blessing," Isabella flashed a quick smile. "But I'm not sure she really meant it." Her red lacquered lips trembled. "She said he must complete his obligation to the Canadian Military to finish his degree and be available for service."

Cate scrunched her eyebrows, trying to deduce what the problem could be.

"It's not that I don't want him to fulfill his obligation, but I thought we might get married this summer." A tear rolled down her cheek while the server returned with their drinks.

"I can promise you that my brother will be faithful to you, if that's what you're worried about," Cate ventured.

"Oh, of course!" Isabella opened her eyes widely. "I don't doubt his loyalty in the least, only I love him so much, that I hate to wait. I thought, perhaps, the Allens might repay the army for his two years at University and finish paying his final two years. I had no idea they would be so heartless as to force him to join the army and possibly die in combat." Isabella's voice failed her and she reached into her handbag for a tissue to wipe her tears.

Cate patted her friend's shoulder. "He may not have to serve overseas or anywhere dangerous," she tried to assure her.

"But you don't know that for sure!" Isabella wailed and then took a large drink of her cocktail. "Why won't the Allens cover for him?"

Cate patted her friend's arm in confusion. "Why should they?" she asked. "They're only friends of ours. They don't have any responsibility for our schooling."

"I thought she was your aunt!" Isabella sobbed and then hiccupped loudly.

"Oh, no! I only call her that sometimes. She was like an aunt to us growing up, and they were such good friends with my family. It's an old fashioned thing, I suppose, but we grew up calling them aunt and uncle. We aren't actually related."

This only made Isabella sob louder. She managed to finish her drink and her entire fruit plate; however, before she excused herself, complaining of a headache and left Cate with the bill. She had just enough money to pay it. She hoped the waitress wouldn't report her for her insufficient tip.

The Allens asked Cate where she would like to have dinner on their final night together. Cate wanted to escape the high prices of the hotel and suggested they go to The Spaghetti Factory and then to a movie. She wanted to take her mind off of her worries for her brother and Isabella.

"Are you sure? I've never even eaten there. There's Le Beaujolais, you know. It's very nice. Some of the best Filet Mignon in the world," Robin kissed her fingers to her lips in a sign of Bon Appetit!

"Thank you," Cate was careful not to insult her hosts. "I just feel like something simple and we'll need to eat more quickly to make the movie."

"I've been dying to see Snow Monster," Gerald said enthusiastically. "I'm so glad you suggested it!" His wife rolled her eyes at him. Cate felt Gerald was relieved to have someone else around who didn't think the best things in life needed to be the most expensive.

The next morning, the Allens drove Cate over to the Tilney residence. Ellie had given Cate the code to get in the privacy gate.

"Wow! I am so excited for you," Robin gushed. "What a great opportunity. I'm so pleased they noticed our little Cate."

"You're sure you want to stay here?" Gerald was more cautious. "You don't have to feel obligated. We could say you were needed back home. You can still back out."

Cate grinned at her friends. "No, I really do want to stay. Ellie and Henry are great."

"What about General Tilney?" Gerald quizzed her. "He's always seemed so severe and focused on his work. I'm not sure if he's the best guardian."

"Oh, relax Gerald. She's almost 18. She won't need a guardian much longer and Henry and Ellie are in their 20's. They can look out for her."

They pulled up to the curved stone driveway. Gerald whistled.

Robin inhaled sharply and put a hand on her chest. "My goodness! This is lovely."

Ellie ran out of the house to greet them and was followed by a man in a suit.

"Welcome!" she said, and hugged Cate. "I'm so glad you've come." Then she shook hands with Robin and Gerald. "Thank you for bringing her. I hope it wasn't too much trouble."

"Not at all. It's our pleasure," Gerald replied.

"This is Gordon," Ellie introduced the man in the suit. "He'll carry in your bags, Cate."

Cate was embarrassed, but allowed the man to take her suitcase. She was relieved that he disappeared once they were in the house.

"Can you stay for coffee?" Ellie asked the Allens. "My father was hoping to meet with you, but he had an emergency at the hotel."

"We'd love to," Robin answered, gazing around the opulent surroundings.

"I hope it isn't anything serious," Gerald said.

Ellie waved his worries away. "He has at least one emergency a day. He's always able to work things out. I'm sure it'll be fine."

Ellie pointed out a few rooms and pieces of art on the way to the morning sitting room. Robin asked a lot of questions and seemed to be lapping up the lavish display. Gerald walked with his hands tucked behind his back, as if he didn't want to damage anything.

The sitting room was set with a silver coffee set – urn, cream, sugar and china cups. Henry was talking on his cell phone in the corner of the room, looking out the window. When he noticed them come in, he quickly ended the conversation and came toward them. Cate noticed he had a look of concern which he forced into an easy smile.

"Ah, the illustrious Allens and their delightful guest, Miss Catherine Morland!" he announced, teasing, and stretched out his hand to Gerald.

"It's good to see you all again."

"This house is incredible!" Robin said. "You must treasure your life here."

Henry arched an eyebrow sardonically, but simply replied, "Indeed. Has my sister told you how much my father wanted to join us? I think he's still hoping to finish up his business in time, but for now, you're stuck with us."

"Nothing too troubling, I hope. I'm feeling the urge to get back to my own business as soon as possible," Gerald rubbed his hands together. "It's hard to be away."

"Our dad would say the same thing. He never really gets away, actually," Ellie said, then pursed her lips, as if she wished she hadn't spoken. "Coffee anyone?"

They all accepted the steaming beverage and a plate of biscotti. While the Allens asked Ellie more questions about the hotel and the house, Henry leaned toward Cate and said quietly,

"I suppose you're expecting some ghostly visitors while you are here," he smirked.

"Oh no," Cate replied, blushing. "That would be silly." She took a sip of the fragrant coffee. "A-are there any ghost stories associated with this house?"

"Well, it's very old, and it has housed many managers and their families over the years. Not to mention the nuns. There are a few."

"Tell me!" Cate said.

Henry clucked his tongue and shook his head. "Now is not the time," he motioned his chin at the Allens. "We don't want your friends to change their minds about your staying with us. Besides, I think the stories are better told by moonlight, don't you?"

"Yes, of course," Cate grinned and felt goose bumps along her arms.

Gerald stood up then. "It is so nice of you to have us for coffee, but we really should be getting home." He reached a hand toward his wife.

"So soon? I'm terribly sorry we've missed General Tilney," Robin said.

"Another time," Henry stood as well. "We'll pass your greetings along."

Robin took her husband's hand and followed Ellie and Henry to the door. Cate followed behind them, gazing at her surroundings. For a moment she wondered if she really belonged and had an urge to go home with the Allens, but she shook off the odd sensation and hugged them goodbye instead.

CHAPTER SIXTEEN

"How would you like to go for a drive?" Henry asked once Cate had been set up in the guest room across from Ellie's.

Ellie looked so excited about the prospect that Cate immediately agreed. "We thought we might take you to our little cottage in the woods," Ellie said softly.

"You have another house?" Cate asked.

"It was our mother's family home. She was born in Banff and lived halfway up a mountain. When her parents died, she inherited the house."

They were seated before a cozy fire in Ellie's sitting room in. It was the ideal place to be on Christmas break with its views of snow-capped mountains, comfortable chairs and good books in every corner.

"She used to take us there a lot when we were children," Ellie explained. "It was her favourite place. I think she wished we could live there, but Dad needed to be close to the hotel."

"It has a koi pond and a tree house," Henry chuckled. "Everything you need for a happy childhood."

Cate was momentarily overwhelmed by the wealth of her friends. Why had they chosen her? She could hardly imagine owning two houses when all she had was a mobile home filled with brothers.

"It. . .it sounds incredible."

Ellie collected a picnic lunch from the kitchen and they brought warm clothes in case they decided to hike around a bit. Henry promised stunning views and secret pathways.

He had an old BMW which he steered expertly up the winding mountain road. It was only about a ten minute drive, but when they pulled into a gravel driveway hidden off the main road, it felt like they'd driven back in time.

Tall Jack Pines rose all around them, making Cate feel like a tiny fairy.

They pulled up to a log cabin, nestled into the trees as if it had grown there. When she stepped out of the car, she noticed the tiny pond had been cleared.

"Our mother loved to skate. This is where she taught us," Ellie said, wistfully.

"It's so perfect," Cate rubbed her mittened hands together, as a chill ran up her spine.

"We have a whole collection of ancient skates," Henry said. "I'm sure we have something your size."

"Come on in," Ellie had unlocked a wooden door with metal reinforcements. The entryway was curved and there were carvings above the doorframe. It was like a grown-up gingerbread house.

A cold draft hit her face.

"I'll just turn up the heat," Henry disappeared down a hallway.

The front room was large with a bay window. A grand piano took up most of the room, but it was edged with comfortable-looking chairs and low book shelves.

"I used to dance here when my mom would play," Ellie said and then laughed shortly. "It's hard to believe I could fit. Here's the kitchen," she motioned to a small room opposite. It was tiny, but cheerful. In fact, it was about the same size as Cate's kitchen at home.

"There's a little den over here, where my Dad has installed some modern conveniences, but he hardly ever comes here now." The den boasted a large window looking out into the trees. A small desk was tucked into the corner, but the room was mainly taken up with books. Cate resisted the temptation to search the titles and curl into the chair to read the day away.

Ellie led her out of the room and down a door-lined hallway. She opened three doors and pointed out her bedroom, Henry's bedroom and the guest room. However, she left a fourth door closed.

"This was my mother's room," she said softly. "We don't go in there anymore."

"But why not?" Cate couldn't help saying. "Don't you want to remember her?"

Henry joined them. "I'm sure you know, Cate, how we never stop remembering her. It was our Dad's teaching. Maybe it was the way he was raised. We were supposed to keep her room just as she left it. As a kind of memorial, I believe."

Cate bit her lip, chastising her curiosity. Did they really never go in?

"It's probably old-fashioned," Ellie put her hand on the doorknob. "We can show you the room if you like."

Cate gazed at her friends and forced herself to be polite. "No, no, really. I don't want to make you uncomfortable. I'm just a guest. This house is incredible."

Ellie took her hand off the door and Cate thought she saw a tiny glimmer of disappointment.

"There, that's getting warmer," Henry took off his gloves. "Should we make some coffee? Or would you rather skate first?"

They decided on the latter while they were still dressed for the outdoors. Cate was amazed by the huge collection of skates in a closet beside the den. They all found a pair that fit and took them outside to a little bench beside the pond. Cate was tucked in between her two friends. She felt an urge to rest her head on Henry's shoulder, but she resisted and tied up her long laces instead.

Henry took her hand to lead her out to the ice. She enjoyed the sensation and was glad the cold gave her an excuse for rosy cheeks. She didn't let on too soon that she was quite a capable skater, but then Henry tagged her and said "You're it!" Years of racing her brothers around rinks paid off and she quickly returned Henry's tag and skated free away from him. He gave up on catching her and tagged his sister instead.

"Come on Henry, it's time to practice our waltz!" Ellie said when the game wound down.

"Really, Ellie? In front of Cate? Do we have to?"

Cate laughed at Henry's response. "Yes, you must. Show me your waltz."

"I used to take figure skating lessons," Ellie explained as she arranged Henry into proper waltz position. "We were always short on dance partners and so I begged Henry to practice with me. He's really quite good."

They started off on the same foot, carving half circles around the pond. Cate stood in the middle and watched. She clapped her hands when they finished. Henry bowed deeply and then held out his hand to her.

"Your turn," he said with authority.

"But I only ever played hockey with my brothers," Cate stammered. "I don't know how. . ."

"If I have to dance with my sister, then you have to dance with me. Besides, the girl part is the easy part, all you have to do is follow."

"Is not!" his sister swatted him with her toque, but Henry skated away and whisked Cate along with him.

Henry wrapped one arm around her waist, took her right hand in his and held her left hand out in front of him. "Left, right, left," he instructed her in waltz tempo.

Cate was pleased to find the dance wasn't hard to pick up with Henry calling out each step. Easier than the dances at the ball, at least.

Ellie applauded once they made one round of the dance. Then, Henry stopped calling out steps and Cate just followed his feet while he chatted.

"You're so much easier to teach than my sister. She always thinks she knows everything."

"Well, if she took skating lessons, she probably does." Cate joked.

"True, but I'd rather make mistakes than have to be continually corrected by my sister."

Cate laughed at his logic. "My brothers probably feel the same way, but too bad for them."

Henry chuckled. "I can't imagine you being a bossy older sister. I guess I really don't know you at all."

Cate knew he was joking, but she couldn't help feeling stung. Was she just imagining that he felt something for her?

Henry seemed to notice her response. He squeezed her hand. "I'm just teasing," he said.

Cate forced a smile up at him. "I know. I just realized how little you actually do know me."

Henry shook his head. "I'm afraid you've got it all wrong, Cate. I know you better than I know almost anyone."

Cate scrunched her forehead. "How is that possible? We only met a week ago."

Henry shrugged. "I knew you immediately." He looked at her intently.

She wanted to ask exactly what he meant, but just then, Ellie interrupted.

"I'm starving. Are you two ready for lunch?"

Cate half-wished that Henry would send his sister in ahead of them, but she let go of his hands instead and skated over to the bench to remove her skates.

They ate thick sandwiches filled with meat, vegetables and spicy mustard. A thermos full of hot tea helped take the chill off the morning. Cate couldn't stop shivering after the skate. It was as if her secret hopes for Henry were possibly real and her body couldn't help but tremble with anticipation. After a selection of squares, they settled in to read in the cozy living room while Henry built up a fire. Cate had brought along her copy of The Thirteenth Tale and was pleased to see that Henry had the same book, but when she started reading, a cellphone rang.

"Yeah . . . okay . . . What about Cate? Okay." The conversation was brief, but Cate noticed a look of understanding between brother and sister. Henry hung up and looked toward her.

"Oh father needs us at the hotel," he said, looking peeved. "It's an emergency. It's always an emergency," he seemed to speak the last sentence to himself while raking his fingers through his hair. "He needs us immediately, of course." He pursed his lips and looked directly at Cate.

"It's terribly rude of us, but we'll need to go back to the hotel now. You can make yourself at home at the house and we'll get back as soon as possible."

Cate felt the sting of tears behind her eyes. Could they not leave the hotel one day while she visited?

"I'm so sorry, Cate," Ellie interjected. "This is not what we planned. I'm afraid this is what life is like at our house."

"No!" Cate forced herself to be bright. "Of course, I understand. It's probably a very busy time of year." She placed her bookmark across her page. "I'll be fine. I'll be happy to read and I'm sure I can take care of myself for the afternoon."

"I don't know how much more of this I can take," Henry muttered to himself while he pushed the logs apart and dampened the fire.

Cate helped Ellie clean up the skates and picnic. It didn't take long to pack up the little house and lock it behind them. Then they were back in the car, winding down the mountain.

Within a few minutes of returning home, Ellie and Henry were dressed in white shirts and blue and green kilts.

"It's a special event," Ellie said sheepishly.

"It's time to bring out the tartans!" Henry said in a heavy Scottish brogue while beating his chest.

"I'm so sorry," Ellie said again.

"Don't worry about it!" Cate said, walking them to the door. "I'm sure I can entertain myself in your beautiful house."

"If you get hungry, just ask Eloise to cook you something. We'll be back in time for a late dinner."

Henry reached for Cate's hands and grasped them dramatically. "Whatever you do, dearest, try not to get completely plastered while we're out." He was still imitating a Scottish warrior.

Ellie rolled her eyes and pulled on her brother's arm. "Come on, Henry. Leave poor Cate alone."

Cate had no desire to be left alone, but she let him go and closed the door behind her friends.

CHAPTER SEVENTEEN

As soon as Henry and Ellie pulled out of the driveway, the house began to feel huge and empty. Cate knew there were several employees still scurrying about the mansion, but she didn't know them. To them, she was a stranger, someone to be suspicious of while their employer was out. She hurried to her room and closed the door behind her.

She read for several hours, until the sun began to dip behind the mountains. Then she stood and stretched, wondering how much longer she would be left alone. She walked around her room, becoming curious of her surroundings and bolder with having been alone within them for so long. The Thirteenth Tale had filled her with questions and possibilities of what might lurk within the old house.

Once she had exhausted the confines of the guest room – a search for long lost love letters had only revealed an old dry-cleaning list – she ventured out into the hallway. At first she just stood beside her door, listening for footsteps. As far as her strained ears could tell, she was all alone on this level. She ventured past her room and paused to study the paintings on the walls. Dark mountain passes and stark winter scenes dominated the artwork. She passed Ellie's room, lingered a moment at Henry's door and moved on to the room she knew had been Ellie's mother's. She put her hand on the doorknob, but then drew it back in alarm. She certainly couldn't go against the wishes of her hosts. They had only been good to her. She listened again for footsteps or voices, but there was only muted silence. Her hand seemed to reach out on its own accord. She was so curious. She turned to walk away, but the mystery of Henry's past tugged on her. On impulse she opened the door, slid inside and pulled it shut behind her.

The room was spotless – she had imagined layers of dust after being sealed so long, but it was clear someone still entered to clean the pretty room. It was much brighter than she had suspected. It was similar to Ellie's room; however, the apartments were significantly larger.

She moved to turn around and leave the room immediately, but her eye caught on a collection of hardcover Nancy Drew books on one of the white, built-in bookshelves. She pulled one off to look through and an envelope dropped to her feet. She bent to pick it up and considered. Should she open the letter? Nancy Drew wouldn't hesitate. Perhaps it contained a long-lost message to Ellie from her mother. She slid it back into the book, but then thought again and quickly opened it to see what was inside.

The brown case.

Midnight

Murder

Cate shivered. What did it mean? The script was almost childish, the paper old and yellowing. Ellie's mother had died nine years ago. Did paper yellow in nine years? Had she hoped her daughter would find the answer to her death? She placed the paper back inside the envelope and turned it around in her hands, but there was no inscription. She placed the message back inside The Clue of the Broken Locket, her hands trembling slightly. She made sure the books were neatly lined up again so no one would know she had pulled the book off the shelf. She could always find it again if she decided to tell her friend.

She stopped to listen again and then continued in her search of the room. She found a collection of small, framed photographs on a low table. General and Mrs. Tilney on their wedding day – she looked a lot like Ellie in a long, frothy gown and he looked surprisingly like his son in a kilt and sporran. Mrs. Tilney was shading her eyes from the sun – it was not a professional photo, and she was not smiling. General Tilney; however, looked triumphant and had a proprietary arm around her shoulders.

The rest of the pictures were of children. Even though they were years younger, Cate identified her friends and marveled at how sweet they seemed. Frederick looked mischievous, even as a toddler, while Ellie looked perfectly composed and Henry always wore a big grin.

She moved to the bedroom then, telling herself to hurry up. She'd been there much too long already and she felt guilty, but she must make sure . . . of what she did not know.

The sheets and comforter on the bed were snow white and perfectly pressed. Brightly-coloured pillows added colour to the pristine room. Two large dressers and a number of comfortable chairs filled out the space along with a dainty vanity set by one of the windows. The brown case stood out like a bruise on the face of a beautiful woman. It was tucked beside the vanity – old and cracked. Cate rushed to it, praying it wasn't locked.

The lid creaked open at her touch and Cate was overwhelmed by the contents. Bundles of letters were tied together with ribbon. Dried flower petals covered the correspondence, giving off a pungent scent of something long lost. Had Mrs. Tilney had another lover? Did her husband become enraged with jealously? Then why would she keep them out in the open this way?

She carefully untied a faded pink ribbon, her hands trembling as she opened the first missive.

"My lovely Genevieve

Your long raven hair has trapped me, my dear. I can think of nothing else. I haven't slept in weeks, dreaming of the next time we should meet."

The letter was difficult to make out – the ink was faded and the penmanship was cramped. Cate rushed to see who had signed at the bottom and read William Drummond. So it was not General Tilney! Her suspicions were confirmed. She hardly knew what to do next. She felt dizzy and slightly faint when she heard the doorknob turn behind her.

She stood up, the letter fluttering to the ground at her feet. There was no time to hide her deeds when Henry strode through the door.

"Cate?" he asked, his face serious for the first time since she had known him. "What are you . . ." He took in the scene before him, seeming to register all she had done and envisioned.

"This is my mother's room," he said, somewhat severely. "My father does not like us to come in here."

"I. . .I'm sorry," Cate stuttered, her mind urging her to make up some story of deceit, but she could not obey. "I was so curious. I wanted to make sure. . ." she could not finish her thought.

"Make sure of what?" Henry looked genuinely perplexed.

"Only, your mother died when no one was at home. I wondered. . . I suspected. . ." her voice trailed off. Her ideas sounded preposterous out loud.

"Suspected?" Henry looked taken aback. "My mother was not home alone. Frederick and I were here. Only Ellie was missing."

"Your father has always seemed so, so, stern. It seemed to me that he was angry about something. . ." She hated the sound of her voice. Tears began to threaten.

"My father is O.C.D." Henry replied. "It's nothing to be proud of. It makes him difficult to live with, but it does not make him a murderer, if that is what you're suspecting."

Cate stared at the letters at her feet, hoping they would give justification to her dark thoughts. "You've found my grandmother's letters," Henry said, slightly less harshly. "They were very precious to my mother, having lost her parents just after we were born."

"Oh," Cate felt shame rushing through her body. "I'm so sorry." She bent to tidy up the letters and quickly closed the case. Then she hurried out of the room, leaving Henry to close the door behind her.

Cate tried to compose herself in her room for fifteen minutes, but she couldn't stop the tears that kept plummeting down her cheeks. She was just patting her face with a cool cloth when she heard a tapping at her door.

"Oh Cate!" Ellie's face turned from joy at seeing her friend to concern. "What's the matter?"

"It's nothing," Cate tried to smile. "Allergies I think."

Ellie's brow furrowed. "We left you too long, didn't we? I'm so sorry."

"No, really. I'm fine."

Cate was relieved that it seemed Henry had not told his sister what she had been up to.

"Are you sure? Your family is alright and everything? You probably miss them, with it being the holidays and everything."

"I'm sure they're fine," Cate shrugged, allowing Ellie to draw her own conclusions.

Ellie bit her lip as if trying to keep her next sentence from coming out. "I should let you have some time to recover, but my Dad is asking that we come for supper. I know we haven't given you any warning, but when he's hungry, we eat. You never know when he's going to get called back to the hotel." She spread her hands out, palm up, as if in apology.

"Oh, that's fine. I'm a little hungry myself," Cate said. "I'll just freshen up a minute."

"I'll wait for you in the hall. I hate to leave you alone anymore."

"Thanks."

The dining room was set with several plates and a myriad of cutlery. There were fresh flowers and elegant long-stemmed crystal glasses. Cate brushed at her jeans and long-sleeved t-shirt, wishing they'd magically turn into evening wear.

"Ah, Miss Morland, how good it is to have you in our home again," General Tilney grasped her hand and then pulled her toward him to kiss her cheek.

"Th-thank you, sir. It's so kind of you to have me."

"Henry was just telling me how much you enjoyed skating up at the old cabin. I never could get a handle on the sport, myself."

"It's a lovely place," Cate said. Henry mustn't have told his father about her other adventure. Still, she couldn't look him in the eye.

"Well, let's eat," General Tilney held out his hand for her plate. She gave it to him and he began heaping roast beef onto the fine china.

When they had finished their first course, General Tilney patted his stomach, sighed and then looked, penetratingly, at Cate. "Cate, there's something I'd like to speak to you about," he said.

She stiffened. Perhaps Henry had told him.

"I'll cut to the chase. I have a manager's apprenticeship program at the hotel. I don't often find someone of your character and obvious talents and I'd hate to lose you."

She scrunched her nose. Talents and character? She hardly knew him.

"I'd like to offer you the opportunity to come work for me this summer. The hotel offers free accommodation for its employees and, through the apprenticeship program, you would be given the best of the rooms. You wouldn't need to share with anyone, you'd have your own kitchen and a sitting room for entertaining guests." He smiled, grandly.

"That's very generous," Cate said.

"You'd work long hours, but I know you would learn quickly and by the end of the summer, I'm sure we could find a more permanent position for you in our hotel."

"I don't know what to say," Cate replied, honestly. She noticed Henry and Ellie trading concerned glances.

"All you need to say is yes, my dear. Your connection to the Allens has prepared you for such opportunities. I imagine Mr. Allen will be quite pleased. I think it would bring our families closer together."

Cate glanced at Ellie. Did she understand what he was talking about? But she had no time to ask. General Tilney's hand was hovering over the soup tureen, waiting for her to reply.

"Thank you, General Tilney. It's a very generous offer. I'll just need to check with my mother, but I'm sure she'll agree."

The General clapped his hands together, smiled and said "Smashing. I'll draw up the paperwork tonight."

Cate's head whirled. She snuck a peek at Henry to see what he thought of the arrangement, but his expression was turned entirely to his bowl of creamy carrot soup. Would he tell his father that he should rethink his offer? How could she be trusted, when she couldn't even keep out of a private room for half a day?

Cate did her best to eat her dinner and a rich pudding afterward. Henry excused himself immediately after they were done and explained he would be driving into Calgary for the night. He had a school project to prepare. Cate was grateful to escape the two men and retire to Ellie's room to play cards and watch a movie.

CHAPTER EIGHTEEN

Cate surprised herself by falling asleep quickly. She'd assumed she'd lay awake, chastising herself for her rudeness, but instead the events of the day had exhausted her. At one in the morning, she sat upright in alarm. Someone was banging on her bedroom door.

She reached for her lamp and hurried to pull on her housecoat and slippers and padded, unsteadily, to the door. When she opened it, she saw Ellie looking completely miserable.

"Cate, I'm so sorry. This is horrible. I can't believe my father. . ."

Cate froze in terror. Had Henry told General Tilney?

"Come in," Cate pulled her friend into the room and they sat together on the couch.

"What's the matter?"

"My Dad, he's insensible," Ellie searched her eyes as if hoping she would understand without having to say the words.

"What is it?" Cate asked, softly.

"He. . ." Ellie chewed her lip. "He's suddenly remembered that he has asked a large party to stay at our house."

"Oh?" Cate was taken aback. Was that all?

"They're expected first thing in the morning."

"So you'll need my room," Cate felt somewhat relieved.

"Yes . . ." Ellie took a deep breath. "But he wants it to be cleared first thing in the morning."

"That's not a problem. I can pack up right away. I don't have a lot, really." Cate stood to begin at once, but Ellie held out her hand to hold her back.

"He wants you to leave tonight," she looked up at her, tears in her eyes. "Within the hour." She dropped her eyes as if in shame. "Oh Cate, this is dreadful. He's taking back his offer for the management apprenticeship too. I have no idea what's gotten into him."

Cate figured she knew. "It's alright," she patted her friend's hand. "I can be ready in half an hour."

Ellie stood up beside her friend. "It's worse," she continued, trembling. "He wants you to take the bus. I can run you to the station, but he doesn't want me to drive at this time of night. Plus, he expects me to entertain his friends in the morning."

"Oh," Cate said again, but this time, without hope.

"I never should have invited you to stay," Ellie said, shaking her head. "I know how crazy my father is. But he suggested it and I liked you so much."

"He suggested it?" Cate asked.

"Yes. I don't know why, but he was quite taken with you. I didn't ask questions, I was just glad for the chance to have a friend over. He's so particular."

"I should start packing," Cate said.

"Can I help?" Ellie said, earnestly.

Cate smiled at her friend and hugged her. "I'll be fine. Don't worry. It's not your fault and I don't blame your father. He's very busy. I'm sure it's easy to forget some of his obligations."

Ellie pursed her lips. "That's what makes this whole thing even worse. I'm nearly positive he just invited these friends to come. He never has guests. I think it's just an excuse." She looked bewildered. "I'll just get dressed and then I'll come back to help."

Cate walked her friend to the door and then rushed to dress, brush her teeth and pack her belongings, tears streaming down her cheeks all the while. Henry must have told him. He would never forgive her. How could she have been such an idiot?

She was ready with time to spare, and the few minutes she waited for her friend to collect her seemed endless and excruciating. It only gave her time to relive her time in Mrs. Tilney's room and especially the look on Henry's face. Over and over again, she remembered his eyes and read more and more disgust into his surprised features.

At last, there was a soft knocking at her door and she grasped her new suitcase.

"The car is ready," Ellie's lip was trembling.

Cate pursed her own and took the lead, carrying her bag down the stairs.

"I should have had someone do that for you," Ellie said, her hand to her mouth. "I could call Gordon right now."

"No, please," Cate's voice was strained. "It's no trouble and I'd rather not wake anyone up."

Ellie followed meekly and at last they were out of the oppressive house into the chill night air.

'You've been such a good friend to me," Ellie chattered constantly as she drove. "My father agreed. He seemed to admire you as much as Henry and I did. I can't understand it. Nothing makes sense."

Cate could offer no comfort to her friend when she knew it was all her fault. "Don't blame your father," she said as they reached the bus station. "I'm sure he had good reason. It's really no problem."

Ellie found a parking space and then turned to Cate, her eyes wide. "I hate to ask you this, it's so personal, but I know you've been away from home longer than you expected and I wonder, do you have enough money for a ticket home?"

Cate was ashamed to admit her answer. She opened her purse and reviewed the small amount of money she had left. "I. . .thank you for asking. No, I don't think so, but I'm sure I can call my mother and arrange to have her pay. . ."

Ellie put her hand over Cate's. "Please don't wake your mother. Would you let me buy your ticket?"

Cate started to shake her head.

"You were our guest. We took you from the Allens, promising to care for you when they hardly knew us. You must allow me to do this one small thing."

Before Cate could answer, Ellie popped open the trunk, grasped Cate's suitcase and hurried inside to the ticket counter.

A Tim Horton's shop emitted a comforting smell in the midst of Cate's restless mind. She left her friend at the counter and moved toward the familiar store to buy herself and her friend a cup of tea.

Ellie joined Cate at a table by the window a few minutes later. "I wasn't sure if you took sugar and cream," she said, motioning at the packets beside Ellie's teacup.

"Thank you," she smiled through her watery eyes.

They sat in silence. Cate was afraid she would give away her awful secret if she opened her mouth at this late hour. Ellie seemed to have used up her words in the car.

"If only Henry were here," Ellie murmured after they had drunk half of their tea. "He's always stood up to Dad, where I've only ever tried to please him. It's impossible, though," she sighed.

Cate clasped her friend's hand. She needed to tell Ellie the truth so she could stop blaming herself. "I . . ." she began.

"Passengers to Canmore, Calgary, Strathmore and Brooks to Gate 7," an overhead voice droned and then repeated itself.

Cate picked up her cup and stood. She hugged her friend. "It was very good to meet you. Don't be too hard on your father. I'm really not good enough for you." Her voice caught. She was no better than the Thorpes with her inability to confess the truth.

"You take that back, Catherine Morland," Ellie hugged her fiercely. "What you are is far too good. I'll find some way to make this up to you."

She smiled sadly in return, but knew it wouldn't be long before Henry told his sister what really happened. She would never see any of them again. And perhaps it would be a relief to be able to forget how stupid she'd been. But she would miss Ellie. . . and Henry.

"Promise you'll call as soon as you make it home," Ellie said to Cate as she boarded the bus.

"I will," Cate said and waved goodbye.

Due to the late hour, Cate was able to secure a seat to herself. She dozed most of the way, waking briefly at each stop. It was still dark when the bus rolled into Strathmore and even though it was now morning, the sun had not yet risen. She collected her suitcase, zipped her jacket and pulled on her mitts and toque. She could not call her mom. She'd face the disgrace in person, not on the phone and so she began walking home.

CHAPTER NINETEEN

All Cate wanted to do when she unlocked the door was climb into bed and stay there. The trailer looked more run down than ever, even though her mother kept it so spotless. Cate chastised herself for thinking it and blamed herself for succumbing to the finery she had lived within for the past week. Had it only been a week? It seemed like she had become a new person since leaving home.

She relocked the door and tiptoed to her bedroom, but her mother opened her door only a moment later.

"Catherine?" she looked confused and disheveled. "What are you doing here?"

Cate's lip trembled as she sat on her childhood bed and her mother sank down beside her. "What is it, my girl?"

"I came home. The Tilneys were expecting some guests." Cate stared at a loose thread on her bed, willing herself not to cry.

"But when did you arrive? How did you get here?"

Cate unzipped her jacket and removed her toque and mittens. "I just walked in the door a few minutes ago. I took the bus."

"And you walked home?" her mom looked horrified.

"No one was out, Mom. It was safe. I didn't want to wake you."

"But why did you have to leave now? It doesn't make any sense. You must have left in the middle of the night." Her mother studied Cate's bedroom clock as if she'd forgotten how to read time.

"They needed my room right away, I guess."

"Rich people," her mother muttered.

"It's not because they're rich," Cate said, but she stopped herself from telling her mother the real reason she had to leave. It was too shameful.

Her mom seemed to shake herself out of her stupor and wrapped her arms around Cate. "I'm so glad you're home," she said, running her hand through Cate's hair. "Next Christmas, you're staying with us."

Cate laughed softly. "Yes, Mom."

Her mom pulled back and looked Cate over. "You must be exhausted. Do you want to eat some breakfast first or just go to bed?"

"Bed," Cate said, glad that she wouldn't have to answer any more questions.

Her mom kissed the top of her head, pulled the blind and padded out of the room. Cate had never appreciated her own bed more.

When Cate awoke again, it was almost noon. Her mom must have bribed her brothers to be quiet. She couldn't remember ever sleeping so late in her life. She had a shower and unpacked her bag before facing her family in the kitchen.

"Cate!" her three younger brothers tackled her when she came into the family room. They were all playing some kind of video game on the family T.V. That must have been how her mom kept them quiet.

"What'd you bring me?" said one.

"What was it like, living in a castle?" shouted another.

"Play with me!" begged the youngest.

Cate hugged each of them, despite their squirms and returned to her room to retrieve the candy she'd bought them. They whooped and unwrapped their treats as fast as she could hand them out. Then her mother demanded they go outside to play.

"I hope they didn't wake you," her mom said once they were all snowpantsed, mittened and out the door.

"Nope. I was dead to the world," Cate grinned.

"Coffee?" her mom asked. Cate accepted gratefully and made herself some toast. Once she had spread peanut butter and jam on each piece, she noticed her mom seemed to be waiting to tell her something.

"What is it?" she asked through a sticky bite.

Her mother sighed and took a sip from her coffee. "Your brother's engagement is off," she said.

"What?" Cate was dumbstruck. "When? Why?"

Her mom spread out her hands in surrender. "I don't know much. I haven't even met her. It's all been so fast and strange. James called last night."

"But Isabella was in love with him. And he seemed to be completely in love with her."

"She broke it off," her mom said.

"But why?"

"James is coming tonight. Maybe he can tell you." She pulled out some cleaning spray and began scrubbing at the kitchen sink. "I suppose it's better that it happened sooner rather than later."

Cate took a bite of toast and chewed thoughtfully. "She was so set on marrying him. I always thought she was rushing things and now she's changed her mind?"

Her mom scrubbed harder. "If we had more money, I'm sure no one would treat my children this way," she said through gritted teeth.

Cate reached out to stop her mother's hand. "Oh, Mom. I'm sorry. I'm sure it had nothing to do with money. It's just two disappointing things in a row. Maybe some relationships aren't meant to be."

Her mom huffed out a breath. "I hope you're right."

"And the Allens have money and they've always treated us well."

Her mom rinsed out her sponge and gave her a weak smile. "You're right. But they're special. We're very lucky to have them."

Both women seemed to sink into their own thoughts while the sounds of screaming and laughing boys drifted into the trailer.

After the conversation with her mother, Cate felt strange calling Ellie, but she had promised and so she dialed the number on her cell phone.

"Hello?" she said.

"Catherine! I've been worried sick. Are you okay?"

Cate was relieved to hear concern in her friend's voice. She had worried she would hear the details of Cate's intrusion, but it seemed she hadn't been told yet.

"I'm fine, yes. I got home early this morning and then I slept in for a while."

"Oh, thank heavens," Ellie let out a breath. "I'm so sorry, Cate. Really this whole thing is so embarrassing."

"It's nothing, really. Don't worry about it. My mom missed me anyway. It's good to be home."

"Well, I am sorry. I'm sure you won't ever trust us again. My father is so... Anyway, I'm glad you're safe."

"Look, don't blame your father. I did something I shouldn't have. I'm really sorry," Cate started.

It's seemed her friend had not heard her. "Oh, Cate, I'm sorry. Dad's calling I have to go. I hope you'll keep in touch. I really enjoyed having you visit."

She promised, but she wondered how long their friendship could last once the truth came out. Cate hung up and offered to help her mother make lunch.

The afternoon dragged on, even though Cate did her best to keep busy. She played the games her brothers had received for Christmas, washed and put away her clothes and helped her mom with dinner. It was a relief when James arrived. Rather than seeming shabby and small, their home became cozy and warm when he entered. He enveloped each of them in bear hugs, chased his brothers around the house and then handed out small gifts.

"This is how it should be all the time," their mother sighed when they sat down to dinner. "If only Dad were here," her lip quivered and all the children were silent for a moment, missing their kind and generous Dad.

Then she took a deep breath and said "James, will you say grace?"

James bowed his head. "Thank you Lord for our family and for bringing us together. Thank you for our Dad watching over us and that we can remember him together. Bless this food and the hands that prepared it. Amen."

The rest of the family echoed his amen and Cate thought how much her brother sounded like their Dad now that he was grown. They passed around the bowls of corn, mashed potatoes and ham. This was the Christmas Dinner she'd been missing. Nothing at all like what she'd eaten at the Banff Springs, but exactly what she was craving.

The boys took up all of James' attention until at last they were tucked into bed. Then James joined Cate and their mom for tea in the living room.

"I sure miss them when I'm gone," James said. "But boy do they wear you out!"

"They're so happy to see you," their Mom said. "They haven't gone so long without fighting since I don't know when."

Cate couldn't make pleasant conversation. She'd been waiting all day to find out and she couldn't wait any longer. "What happened with Isabella? I thought she was crazy about you."

James' face grew hard. "She seems to have a short attention span. I thought she was too, but once she met Fred Tilney, her passions took a turn," he said drily.

"Henry's brother?"

"Tilney? What kind of people are they? They seem to be out to make our lives miserable," their mother spat.

"It isn't the Tilneys. Not Henry and Ellie, at least. Even their father can't be blamed. . ." She left the sentence hanging, unfinished. She couldn't tell them the rest.

"It's not like he stole her away from me," James passed a hand over eyes that looked weary. "I guess I didn't really know her all that well. She seemed to be throwing herself at him. I tried not to mind. I didn't want to seem jealous and possessive, but my feelings were too real. I had every reason to feel jealous. She told me she didn't love me anymore."

"Oh, James," Cate and her Mom said at the same time and then wrapped their arms around his shoulders.

"She wasn't nearly good enough for you," Cate said. "I can't believe I thought she was my friend."

James sighed. "I don't think she meant to be such a jerk," he said. "I don't think she really understands other people's feelings. I didn't see that before, but things started to add up once she broke it off, the way she didn't care if you'd made plans with the Tilneys, how impulsive she was. . ."

"That's it," their mother interjected. "You two will just have to stay home with me forever. I can't protect you when you go out into the world."

James and Cate chuckled. "Ah, Mom." James kissed the top of her head.

They were all too worn out to do or say much else. They settled in to watch Seinfeld reruns for the rest of the evening.

CHAPTER TWENTY

James decided it was time the boys burned off some energy. It was freezing, below 20°C, but they were used to it. Winter in Alberta was a long, cold affair. Cate didn't feel like going, but the pleading of all of her brothers got her into her snow gear and out the door.

"Dinosaur Hill! Dinosaur Hill!" her younger brothers had made up a chant as they walked. Cate joined in. It made her warmer.

They dragged all types of snow riders behind them. James had given them some new racers; they also carried toboggans, crazy carpets and a well-used plastic snowboard. "I wanna go fast!" said Levi, the youngest. Cate rubbed his toqued head and promised he would.

The hill was busy, despite the cold. They had received 10 centimetres of fresh snow the night before and children who had been home from school for Christmas holidays were anxious to break it in. Dinosaur Hill was a large green space surrounded by fenced homes which echoed back the laughter and squeals from the hill.

Cate embraced the chance to play with her brothers after all of her recent rejection and embarrassment. It was good to see James smile as well.

After an hour, they were wet and chilled. James carried Levi on his shoulders while Cate dragged most of the sleds behind her. They piled into the house and were greeted by the Allens.

"Hello!" Robin called to them with outstretched arms. The boys obediently submitted to her hugs.

Their mom had hot chocolate, coffee and cookies prepared. The Allens asked all about their afternoon adventure and laughed at the boys' epic tales. Once they had told their stories and taken care of the snack, they disappeared to play video games and Robin turned her attention to Cate.

"Your mother told us about your hurried departure from the Tilneys, but I just can't believe it. What on earth happened?"

Cate's stomach turned. The last thing she wanted was to talk about it again. "General Tilney was expecting some company he'd forgotten about. They needed my room right away, so I took the bus home." She tried to be succinct.

"It's hardly acceptable to send a young woman home in the middle of the night on a bus," Gerald pounded a fist on the table. "I can't believe how poorly I judged him."

"He was so friendly when we met," Robin turned to their mother. "So eager to have Catherine stay with his daughter. I got the feeling she didn't have a lot of friends."

"Well, no wonder when her father treats them like this," Gerald's voice rose.

"It really wasn't that bad," Cate tried to cover for his actions. "He meant no harm. I was in absolutely no danger and now I get to spend more time with my family."

Just then, the doorbell rang and Cate was relieved to have the attention drawn away from her and breathed deeply for the first time since returning home. James answered the door and all conversation ceased when he said "Henry!" in surprise.

He wore a long black jacket and woolen toque. His cheeks were red from the cold and Cate thought he had never looked more handsome. She half-rose to greet him, but then sat down again, her knees weak.

He removed his hat and James closed the door. "Good afternoon," he said. "I'm sorry to show up unannounced like this. I tried to call Catherine's cell, but there was no answer."

Cate remembered she had left her phone on her bed stand after speaking to Ellie. She hadn't charged it since she'd come home and it was probably dead. "How did you find us?" she blurted.

"Ellie gave me your address," he said.

"Would you like some coffee?" Cate's mother interjected. Cate noticed the welcome in her mother's tone. Apparently she didn't blame Henry for his father's bad manners.

Cate introduced her mother to Henry and he shook her hand firmly. "I'm so sorry for the way Cate was treated," Henry's voice sounded controlled, as if he were holding back some strong emotion. "I came as soon as I heard. I had no idea."

"Thank you," her mother nodded.

The Allens questioned Henry about his drive through the new snow and asked him where he'd come from. Cate couldn't say anything, but watched his every move. What did his smile mean? The tightness around his mouth. Were his hands shaking with cold or something else?

Once he'd drunk his coffee and made an acceptable amount of small talk with everyone at the table, his eyes settled on Cate. "I know she's just returned, but would you mind if I took Cate out for dinner? I promise to have her back at a decent hour," something of Henry's humour had returned to his voice and features.

"Of course," Cate's mother said.

Cate hurried to change out of her tobogganing clothes and put on some makeup. Her hand shook as she applied eyeliner and she had to wipe it off and try again.

"You look lovely," Robin said when Cate said goodbye. "Enjoy yourselves!" she waved.

Cate forced herself to speak as soon as they were in the car, away from all prying eyes and ears. "Your father must be so angry with me. I had no right to go into your mother's room. I'm so sorry!" she was near tears.

Henry had just turned on to the main road. He took one hand off the steering wheel to grasp hers. He glanced at her a moment, and then said "I didn't tell my father anything. He has no intelligent reason to be upset with you." She noticed his grip tighten on the steering wheel. "My father sent you away because you aren't rich." His lips were a thin line.

Catherine scrunched her brow. "I never was or claimed to be. I think it's pretty obvious that I'm not."

"It was your friend, John Thorpe." Henry replied.

"John Thorpe has never been my friend," Cate studied Henry's face. "What does he have to do with this?"

"Apparently, he told my father that you would inherit all of the Allens' property and hotels. He said they were training you to take over their business – since you were their niece."

"But I'm not their niece," Cate was confused and then she remembered her first meeting with Isabella and with Henry. "Ohh. I called Robin my Aunt. It's been a family tradition. We were so close. . ."

"It has nothing to do with you. I'm sure Thorpe was bragging to my Dad about you to impress him. He must have known you weren't related. He's friends with your brother, but Dad fell for it. He was hoping for a partnership between the two hotel chains. Perhaps even a take-over."

"Well." Cate didn't know what to say. They had pulled into the parking lot of the nicest restaurant in town. The building had been made to look like a large train station. Streetlamps shone on the fresh snow.

Henry let the car run and turned to Cate to take both of her hands in his. "You have every reason to hate my family. I wouldn't blame you if you wanted nothing to do with any of us, but unfortunately, I'm extremely attracted to you," he looked at her, his brown eyes warm and hopeful.

"You are? But I was such an idiot." Cate felt a fresh wave of shame over her snooping.

"Who could blame you?" Henry shrugged. "Our family is completely neurotic. You must have had all kinds of questions. All you really did was go into a room and look around."

Cate laughed nervously. "Well, when you put it that way. . ."

Henry let go of her hands and rubbed his temples. "And then there's my brother." He looked disgusted. "I can't believe Isabella turned down James to be with him. He's already dumped her for someone else. He's a total mimbo."

"Seriously? Why didn't you warn me?"

"I didn't think I needed to. I thought any friend of yours would have more sense than to fall for Freddy."

Despite this bad news for her brother, Cate's mind was stuck on the fact that Henry was interested in her. Silence hung in the warm car until he reached out a hand to touch her cheek. He pulled her toward him and kissed her, surprising her with his intensity. With all of his jokes and sarcasm, she'd never guessed he felt like this. She kissed him back with delight, realizing all the feelings she'd been denying. He was exactly who she wanted.

"Do you think you could like me?" Henry asked when they pulled away from one another.

Cate felt herself blush at his direct question and gaze. "What about your dad?"

"I already told him off," Henry said. "My father needs me. I made him swear to apologize to you. Expect a call tomorrow."

"That's not really necessary."

"Yes it is!" Henry insisted. "No one's going to treat my girlfriend like that. You have every reason to deny forgiving him."

Cate kissed Henry again. "Don't be ridiculous. I'm not your girlfriend yet."

Henry suddenly grew pale.

"I'm joking!" she said, holding up her hands in surrender. "And of course I'll forgive your father, but you owe me a ghost story before I become your girlfriend. Come on, let's go inside."

They found the most secluded table in the busy restaurant by a window in the corner. Cate ordered a wine while Henry sat ruminating over a pint. She was beginning to worry over his silence when he finally began.

"When I was a boy, I used to have trouble sleeping in our big house. On windy nights, there was creaking and whistling in the attic. Sometimes I'd crawl into my parent's bed, but my Dad would always carry me back to my own room.

"'Big boys do not sleep with their Mommy's and Daddy's,' he'd say.

"After one such incident, I sat at a chair by my window, upset with my Dad for being so heartless. There was fresh snow on the ground, not unlike tonight," Henry turned to look out the window and Cate followed his gaze.

"There was a full moon and it seemed almost as light as day to me. I decided to put on my snow gear and go outside. I was not going to sleep if I couldn't be with my mom."

"What a little rascal you were," Cate interjected.

Henry narrowed his eyes and stared into the bottom of his glass while he paused to drink. Then he moved his chair closer to Cate and grasped her hands in his.

"I've only ever told this story to Ellie. I thought Fred would laugh and I could never admit this to my Dad."

"What about your mom?" Cate asked, enjoying his nearness.

"I didn't want to frighten her. I'm not sure I should frighten you." Henry raised his eyebrows like a question mark.

Cate took a gulp of wine, hoping to warm the chill that was creeping up her neck. "If you could tell your little sister, I'm sure I can handle it."

"I warned you." Henry shrugged. "I found footprints in the snow when I snuck out. I had nothing else to do but follow then. I heard crying near the river, so I continued on. A small part of me hoped it was my mother, sorry that she couldn't let me stay near to her.

"Then in a thicket of trees, I saw a dark figure."

Cate couldn't disguise a quick intake of breath.

"Are you sure I can go on?"

Cate glared at him. "Quit stalling."

Henry grinned and drew closer, gently caressing her hair and tucking it behind her ear. Then he started to whisper, sending shivers throughout her body.

"She was one of the nuns from our own abbey," he paused to study Cate, curling a strand of hair in his finger. Cate tried to hide her unease.

"Her name was Annette. French. Far from home. She beckoned for me to come closer.

"I did, of course. She was stunning. Raven-haired with pale skin. She looked like the moon itself come to life. But when I took her hand, her image wavered. All I heard her say was "Too late."

Cate stared at him. Then she shoved him with her elbow. "She did not. You're making this whole thing up."

Henry pulled away and took another drink. "You can think what you will. But I would still like you to be my girlfriend."

Cate laughed, her heart pounding, but she wasn't sure if it was from fright or excitement when she agreed.

EPILOGUE

As much as John had been making up stories to impress Captain Tilney, he wasn't completely off. When Cate Morland graduated from high school that spring, her family friends, the Allens, presented her with the gift of paying for her tuition. They told her she was at liberty to study anything she wanted, but after spending weekends with Henry at the hotel, she had developed quite an interest in the industry. That fall, she enrolled in hotel management at the same school where Henry studied art. They married only two weeks after graduating and the Allens asked Cate to manage their finest hotel in the city while Henry taught at the college and ran a small gallery downtown.

James completed his studies and was a frequent visitor to Cate and Henry. He and Eleanor became close and found themselves in love just as James was shipped overseas. He returned a different man, but Ellie stayed with him, offering him the kindness and friendship he needed to recuperate. They married a year later and moved away from General Tilney. He was left to live alone with his wayward son, Fred. Much of his time and energy went into paying for Fred's rehab and getting him out of dangerous relationships with married women.

Cate's little brothers visited her and Henry often. They took over the little cabin in Banff, spending most of their weekends and holidays together there, reading thrilling books. Cate was never sure if Henry's ghost story was true, but she kept that little secret to herself.

OTHER BOOKS BY SAMANTHA ADKINS

Expectations: A Continuation of Pride and Prejudice
Suspiciously Reserved: A Twist on Jane Austen's Emma
Defacing Poetry
Subgirl
Subgirl Returns
Not As They Appear

Made in the USA
Charleston, SC
23 June 2016